I Want To Be
An Explorer...

I0641442

I Want To Be
An Explorer...

By

Brett Shayler

BRETT SHAYLER

I WANT TO BE AN EXPLORER...

Forward

By Richard Wiese

President, The Explorers Club

Every explorer's journey begins not with a passport, but with a spark of inspiration. Sometimes it's found in a jungle or on a mountaintop—but more often, it starts in a backyard, a whisper from a willow, or a daring leap off a swing set transformed into a pirate ship.

I Want to Be an Explorer is a celebration of that spark—of curiosity, courage, and the joy of discovering the world through a child's eyes. Jessica's journey reminds us that true exploration isn't just about remote places. It's about perspective. It's about choosing to see the magic in the familiar, the wonder in the everyday.

As President of The Explorers Club, I've met astronauts, deep-ocean divers, and scientists who have traveled to Earth's most extreme environments. But they all share one trait with Jessica: they began with a question, a dream, and a sense of joyful possibility. That same spark lives in every child who turns a blanket into a tent, a stick into a telescope, or a backyard into a kingdom.

Jessica's kindness, creativity, and adventurous spirit remind us that exploring the natural world leads not only to knowledge, but also to empathy and connection. That's the heart of exploration—not just learning about the world, but caring deeply for it.

May this story inspire young minds to wonder, to wander, and to believe that discovery can begin anywhere. Because the greatest explorers aren't always those who go the farthest—but those who look the closest, listen the deepest, and dream the most vividly.

Dedication

I dedicate this book to children whose imaginations transform blades of grass into jungles, trees into mountains, and puddles into oceans. I dedicate this book to those who transform the ordinary into the extraordinary with the sheer force of their imaginations. This is for the dreamers, the explorers, and the adventurers who build worlds in their backyards, on their bedroom floors, and in the quiet corners of their hearts.

This story revolves around a young girl who, instead of seeing adventurers conquering mountains in a documentary, saw a path to her limitless potential. It's for the brave souls who talk to their hamsters, negotiate with butterflies, and build friendships with the wind, whispering secrets. For those who believe a whispered willow tree secret unlocks a hidden cave of glowing crystals: This is for you.

This explains simple wonders for children, such as smooth river stones, colorful seashells, and a grandmother's hug. Children who understand that friends, neighbors, family, and self-belief are the most remarkable treasures, not chests or caves, will appreciate this.

Dedicated to storytelling's power, community's magic, and the enduring spirit of adventure dormant within us, waiting to be awakened by an idea's spark, a dream's whisper, or an imaginative heart's boundless expanse. May this story inspire you to explore the worlds you create, cherish your connections, and always believe in the extraordinary power of your unique imagination. The most incredible adventures are the ones we create ourselves.

Chapter 1: Jessica's Documentary Discovery

Jessica stood still, intently watching the television screen. The documentary, a vibrant tapestry of breathtaking landscapes and daring feats, unfolded before her. Mesmerized, she watched intrepid explorers scale sheer cliffs, their ropes swaying against jagged peaks that pierced a cloudy sky. Then, the scene shifted to a lush jungle, teeming with exotic birds and chattering monkeys, where explorers hacked their way through dense undergrowth, their machetes flashing in the dappled sunlight. Each scene was a feast for her eight-year-old's imagination.

They weren't just explorers but adventurers, pioneers, and heroes charting unknown territories. They were fearless, resourceful, and brimming with a spirit of discovery that ignited something deep within Jessica. She'd always had a vivid imagination, transforming her bedroom into a castle, her blankets into royal robes, and her stuffed animals into loyal knights. But this documentary was unlike anything else.

Though faced with challenges, including rugged terrain, unpredictable weather, and the unknown, the explorers persevered with determination and an unwavering spirit. They faced their fears, celebrated their successes, and learned from their mistakes, all while pushing the boundaries of what was possible. Their resilience and unyielding pursuit of knowledge and experience captivated Jessica.

As the documentary concluded, something stirred inside her, aching and bright. She desired the exhilaration, the triumph, the novelty. She yearned to explore uncharted territories, face her challenges, and uncover hidden wonders. Where could she find this adventure? Her quiet suburban street, with its neat lawns and friendly neighbors, seemed a far cry from the dramatic landscapes shown on the screen. But maybe adventure wasn't about location; perhaps it was about perspective.

A mischievous grin spread across her face as an idea took root. Her backyard, a space for playing hopscotch and chasing butterflies, shimmered with potential. The oak tree at the yard's edge, providing shade, was a tall structure with its branches extending upward. The old swing set, often neglected, became a magnificent pirate ship, ready for daring voyages across imaginary seas. And the flowerbeds, places for pretty blooms, morphed into a dense, exotic jungle, full of hidden pathways and unexpected creatures.

The change began before she even realized it had started. Fueled by a sudden spark of inspiration, Jessica grabbed a collection of colorful scarves and lengths of fabric from her craft box. She draped them over the oak tree's branches, creating vibrant banners fluttering in the gentle breeze. Using a large sheet secured with sturdy rope, she fashioned a makeshift sail for her swing set. She constructed winding paths through her flowerbeds, using twigs and leaves to weave an intricate maze of natural obstacles.

Her pet hamster, Whiskers — a tiny ball of fluffy brown fur with surprisingly curious eyes — watched intently, almost as if understanding every move of the transformation with wide-eyed fascination. He scurried from one newly created landmark to another, his tiny claws clicking against the makeshift pathways. He seemed to understand the magic Jessica was making, his little whiskers twitching as he explored the unfamiliar landscape. She decided he would become her first loyal companion on this exciting journey.

She added finishing touches—a miniature map drawn on a piece of cardboard, marked with cryptic symbols and exciting destinations; a set of small, smooth stones painted with vibrant colors, each representing a different landmark in her newly created world; and a treasure chest crafted from an old shoebox decorated with glitter and stickers. Each element transformed from mundane to extraordinary through the infusion of wonder.

As dusk settled, casting long shadows across her backyard, Jessica stood back and admired her handiwork. Her ordinary backyard had transformed into a fantastical world, a vibrant tapestry of imagination woven from the threads of a documentary and her boundless creativity. She felt a thrill course through her; the adventure had begun. She was no longer Jessica, a girl in a quiet suburb; she was an intrepid explorer, ready to navigate her uncharted territories, with her loyal companion, Whiskers, by her side. The whispering willows, the babbling brook, the towering oak-mountain, and the pirate swing set ship all awaited.

I WANT TO BE AN EXPLORER...

Emulating the documentary's explorers, she met challenges head-on. Her spirit buzzed with something uncontainable—wonder, courage, or maybe both. The journey had begun, and the world, her backyard, was her oyster.

Chapter 2: The Backyard Transformation Begins

The first order of business was the oak tree, a majestic giant that had always provided welcome shade on hot summer afternoons. Now, it was to be Mount Whispering Pines, the highest peak in her christened Backyard Kingdom. Jessica rummaged through her craft box, a treasure trove of colorful ribbons, scraps of fabric, and shaped buttons. She unearthed a roll of shimmering gold crepe paper, perfect for creating the illusion of sunlight glinting off the mountain's rocky slopes. She draped the paper around the thickest branches, securing it with twine and using clothespins to create a cascade of golden light emanating from the tree's heart.

Next came the foliage. Using vibrant green and brown felt scraps, she cut and layered them to create a realistic texture, adding depth and dimension to the mountain's slopes. Adding a splash of unexpected vibrancy, she incorporated some of her mother's old, discarded scarves, bringing a rich color palette to the mix. She attached these to the branches with small safety pins, creating the effect of lush vegetation clinging to the mountain's sides. She used a few branches and crafted the waterfalls from shimmering blue and silver fabric, draping and fastening them to mimic the look of water cascading down the mountainside.

Whiskers, her hamster, observed this creation with keen interest. His tiny nose twitched as he followed Jessica's every move, seeming to grasp the magic she was weaving. His small paws padded across the grass as he ventured closer, and his beady eyes reflected the shimmering gold and green of her handiwork.

He'd sniff the fabrics, his head tilted, as if he were testing the mountain's new features. Jessica chuckled, knowing he was her first official expeditionary companion who would record the transformation in his little hamster way. She created a tiny hammock from a green leaf, hanging it from a lower branch as a rest stop for her intrepid furry explorer.

The swing set, a place for quiet contemplation and gentle swaying, transformed into the formidable "Sea Serpent's Revenge," a fearsome pirate ship ready to sail the uncharted waters of her backyard "ocean"—the lush green lawn. The old, rusty chains became sturdy rigging, and the wooden planks, weathered by time and sun, became the deck of a vessel poised for adventure. Jessica found a large, discarded sheet, its faded floral pattern now adding a touch of quirky charm to the ship's sail. With the help of a sturdy rope, she secured it to the top bar of the swing set, allowing it to billow in the gentle afternoon breeze. She added details, creating a tattered flag from a colorful piece of fabric and adorning the sides with miniature pirate flags fashioned from bits of colored card.

The flowerbeds, a vibrant display of colorful blooms, transformed into the dense, mysterious jungle of Whispering Blooms. Using twigs and leaves collected during her neighborhood walks, she crafted a network of winding paths that wove a maze through the vibrant flowers. She added more scarves, draping them over the bushes to create the effect of dense undergrowth, providing shelter for the imaginary creatures that inhabited this enchanted space.

Small stones, painted with vibrant colors and intricate designs, served as markers guiding the way through the jungle's hidden passages. She even constructed a tiny bridge over a "raging river"—a shallow ditch that ran through the garden—using small sticks and pebbles, showcasing the true essence of a creative builder.

The cave under the porch, a dark and dusty place, became the Crystal Grotto, a mystical cavern filled with shimmering gems. Jessica used various reflective materials she found around the house—broken pieces of mirror, shiny foil, and iridescent cellophane—to create a dazzling display of light. The effect was mesmerizing, turning the small space into a sparkling crystal treasure trove, illuminating the cave with a mystical glow. It was a perfect resting point for her upcoming journey. She placed a small battery-operated lantern inside, emitting a soft light.

As the sun dipped below the horizon, casting long shadows across her transformed backyard, Jessica stood back to survey her work. The ordinary had become extraordinary. She had imbued the familiar with magic. Her backyard was no longer a space for playing; it was a kingdom of adventure, a world waiting to be explored. The towering Mount Whispering Pines loomed large, its golden slopes shimmering in the fading light. The Sea Serpent's Revenge, her majestic pirate ship, stood ready for a voyage into the unknown. And the Jungle of Whispering Blooms, with its winding paths and hidden secrets, beckoned with the promise of discovery.

Even Whiskers, nestled in his leaf hammock on Mount Whispering Pines, seemed to understand the profound transformation that had taken place. He twitched his whiskers, perhaps sensing the thrill of the adventure ahead, his tiny heart full of anticipation.

Jessica felt a thrill that mirrored the sensations she had experienced while watching the explorers on television. She wasn't playing; she was embarking on a true adventure. Her chest tightened, breath shallow with excitement as she prepared for her first expedition. She took her map, made from cardboard with symbols and destinations marked on it, and tied it around her neck with twine.

She tucked her painted stones, each a landmark from her imagined world, into the pouch at her waist. Her treasure chest, filled with imagined riches, rested at her feet.

Her vision's boundless power had transformed the once familiar backyard into an expansive and mysterious world. Encouraged by whispering willows, a babbling brook (a cleverly diverted garden hose), singing adventure, and a towering oak mountain challenging her to reach its summit, she felt inspired. The beckoning pirate ship promised daring voyages across uncharted seas, while the jungle hinted at untold secrets and hidden wonders. It was more than a transformation; it was an invitation to explore, discover, and, most importantly, believe in the magic within her heart and the world around her.

Her grandmother smiled, noticing her granddaughter's intense focus and the dramatic changes in the backyard. Nurturing her imagination as a child, she came to understand its power. She always encouraged Jessica's creative spirit, who often took part in imaginative games, adding wisdom and gentle guidance to the child's fantastical adventures. With a smile, she watched Jessica adjust the makeshift waterfall cascading down Mount Whispering Pines. It was a journey of self-discovery, not a game, that showed Jessica's growing confidence and ability to create her world.

Jessica's mother, while concerned about the chaotic transformation of the backyard, recognized the depth of her daughter's creativity and the joy it brought her. Recognizing imaginative play as crucial to development, she always encouraged Jessica. She provided practical suggestions and gentle encouragement, joining the adventure to assist Jessica with some of the more challenging tasks. With her help, they secured the makeshift sail on the pirate ship and then crafted a small, functional flagpole for the ship's new flag. Her participation wasn't about helping; it was about sharing in Jessica's dream.

The extraordinary changes captivated the friendly immigrant neighbors, who shared childhood memories and tales of adventure, weaving their cultures into Jessica's rich, imaginative world. The older gentleman next door, a retired carpenter, offered his expertise in securing the rope that held up the ship's sail, admiring Jessica's resourcefulness and creativity. The family across the street, from another country, shared tales of legendary creatures from their homeland, adding a touch of fantasy to Jessica's imaginative world.

As darkness enveloped the backyard, the transformation was complete. The moon, a silent observer, cast its gentle glow over the scene, highlighting the mountain's shimmering gold, the ship's billowing sail, and the jungle's winding paths. Jessica stood, surrounded by her creation, a radiant smile lighting up her face. The adventure was about to begin, a journey that would lead her through her backyard and into the deeper realms of her imagination, a testament to the boundless power of childhood creativity and the transformative magic of believing in oneself. And Whiskers, her loyal companion, twitched his whiskers, ready for his first adventure in this wondrous new world. The whispers of the willows, the gurgling brook, and the rustling leaves all seemed to applaud her, their quiet voices mingling with the excitement bubbling within her heart. She had begun her journey, promising an adventure filled with wonder, discovery, and the unwavering belief in the power of her imagination.

Chapter 3: Meeting Whiskers the Adventurous Hamster

Whiskers, a Syrian hamster with an adventurous spirit for his kind, stirred in his tiny, custom-built leaf hammock. He wasn't your average hamster, content with the simple pleasures of sunflower seeds and wheel-running. Oh no, Whiskers possessed a spirit of exploration that mirrored Jessica's own. Whiskers had watched intently, almost as if understanding every move with keen interest as the backyard transformed. The rustling of fabrics, the clatter of stones, and the careful arrangement of twigs—all registered in his tiny, perceptive brain. He had tasted a few stray pieces of felt, the green ones being palatable.

Jessica noticed Whisker's eager movements as she prepared for her first expedition. He was vibrating with anticipation, his little nose twitching as he scurried down the makeshift "mountain," his tiny claws finding purchase on the crepe paper and felt. He recognized the place as an adventure land, not just a backyard. Jessica chuckled, grabbing a miniature backpack she had fashioned from a colorful scrap of fabric. It was too big for Whiskers, but she clipped it onto his tiny harness, which she'd fashioned from a thin ribbon. Inside, she placed a miniature water bottle (a repurposed medicine vial) and a small bag of selected sunflower seeds, each representing a different "landmark" on her map.

"Ready for your first expedition, Whiskers?" she whispered, her voice filled with excitement and a touch of nervous energy. A tiny squeak, Whiskers' reply, Jessica took as enthusiastic agreement. With that, she set off, Whiskers trotting at her side, his little paws padding on the ground.

Their first destination was Mount Whispering Pines. The climb posed a great danger, especially for whiskers. The crepe paper mountain, though stunning, presented a rather challenging climb for a small hamster. Jessica had to guide him, lifting him over steep slopes and securing him with a gentle hand whenever he seemed to lose his footing. Whiskers, however, never complained. He seemed to relish the trial with hidden stakes, his tiny legs working, his determination unwavering.

Along the way, they encountered various obstacles. A precarious section required Jessica to create a makeshift bridge using twigs and leaves, a miniature engineering feat that impressed Whiskers. They also had a close encounter with a ladybug, a fierce predator in Whiskers' eyes, but Jessica's careful intervention prevented any unwanted hamster-related incidents. They found a tiny, concealed cave hidden behind a massive root.

From the summit of Mount Whispering Pines, one could see a breathtaking view of the transformed backyard. On the "ocean," Jessica's pirate ship, The Sea Serpent's Revenge, bobbed, its tattered sail billowing in the wind, whispered secrets. Jessica's colorful markers punctuated the dense, vibrant green expanse of the Jungle of Whispering Blooms far below. Beckoning further exploration, the Crystal Grotto shimmered under the afternoon sun, its mystical glow apparent. Whiskers, perched on Jessica's shoulder, squeaked, his tiny claws digging into her shirt.

From Mount Whispering Pines, they embarked on a journey through the Jungle of Whispering Blooms. The maze-like paths, created by intertwined twigs and leaves, proved challenging, even for Jessica. Still, Whiskers, with his keen sense of smell and uncanny ability to navigate through tight spaces, proved to be an invaluable guide. Jessica followed his lead, sometimes crawling on her hands and knees, sometimes squeezing through the narrow gaps between leaves and flowers. The jungle was teeming with life–butterflies flitted among the flowers, bees buzzed, and ants marched along their paths. Whiskers, however, was only interested in exploring, ignoring the other insects around him.

At one point, they stumbled upon a small clearing, where a hidden treasure awaited—a single, smooth, iridescent blue pebble. Jessica added it to her collection, placing it in her pouch. Whiskers received his reward–a huge and juicy sunflower seed, a prize well-earned for his navigational prowess.

Their expedition continued to the Sea Serpent's Revenge, where Whiskers explored the ship's deck, his tiny paws padding across the weathered wood. He seemed fascinated by the tattered sail, sniffing at it before venturing into the ship's "cabin"–a small, shaded area under the swing set. Jessica, amused by his bravery, let him explore at his leisure, offering him more sunflower seeds as an expression of appreciation for his incredible performance.

Their journey concluded at the Crystal Grotto. The light filtering through the broken mirrors and cellophane cast an ethereal glow on the cave's walls. Whiskers, cautious at first, ventured into the cave, his whiskers twitching as he explored the shimmering crystals. He seemed captivated by their brilliance, his tiny eyes reflecting their dazzling light. As the sun set, casting long shadows across the backyard, Jessica and Whiskers returned to their starting point, exhausted but exhilarated. Their first expedition had been a resounding success.

Whiskers, nestled in Jessica's hands, had proven to be the perfect companion, and his small size and adventurous spirit added a unique dimension to their journey. He explored the backyard, becoming central to the adventure. The day's adventure, a cherished memory, proves that the smallest creatures inspire adventure and reveal the extraordinary in the ordinary. Jessica smiled as she tucked Whiskers into his leaf hammock for the night. Their journey was far from over; the Backyard Kingdom held many more secrets and adventures waiting to be uncovered, all with Whiskers, the adventurous hamster, by her side.

Chapter 4: Whispering Willows and the Hidden River

The sun dipped lower, casting long shadows across the transformed backyard, painting the crepe-paper mountains in hues of orange and purple. The thrill of their successful expedition still buzzing within her, Jessica turned her attention towards a new area of her kingdom—a cluster of weeping willows at the edge of the "jungle." There weren't any willows but the Whispering Willows, their branches draped low to the ground like emerald curtains, creating a mystical, hushed atmosphere.

A faint trickle of water, audible over the chirping of crickets, caught her attention. Peeking beneath the weeping branches, she uncovered a tiny stream, no wider than her hand, winding its way through the roots of the trees. It was a hidden river, a secret waterway flowing through the heart of her backyard kingdom. The crystal-clear water gurgled as it tumbled over smooth stones, creating a mesmerizing melody that seemed to whisper secrets only the willows could understand.

The willows seemed to sway in a silent conversation, their leaves rustling like hushed whispers carried on a gentle breeze. Jessica felt an irresistible pull towards the river, a sense of mystery and adventure beckoning her. She kneeled, cupping her hands to drink from the refreshing water. It tasted like sunshine and turned earth, a taste she couldn't quite place but found captivating.

As she traced the river's course with her fingers, her eyes fell upon something nestled amongst the willow roots—a smooth, gray stone, almost perfectly round. It was unlike any other stone in the backyard, its surface polished, as if the constant flow of water had smoothed it. And then she saw a series of intricate carvings etched into its surface, a cryptic puzzle that tested both heart and mind, waiting to be deciphered.

The carvings were ancient-looking, like hieroglyphics from a long-lost civilization. They depicted a series of symbols—a sun, a moon, a bird in flight, and a winding path leading to a star. Beneath the symbols, someone etched a single word in a familiar yet foreign script: "Solve." This was it, her first actual trial with hidden stakes in the Backyard Kingdom. It was a gateway, a test of wit and ingenuity that would unlock further secrets of her magical realm.

For the next hour, she examined the stone, tracing the symbols with her fingertip to decipher their meaning. She thought back to the nature documentaries she had watched, to the ancient civilizations and their fascinating systems of communication. She reasoned that the sun and moon represented day and night. The bird in flight symbolized freedom and journey. That winding path: It must be the path she needed to follow. But what did the star represent? How did these elements solve the complex puzzle, challenging intellect and emotion?

Her grandmother's words about observation and finding connections between disparate things came back to her. The whispering willows and gurgling river calmed her mind and sharpened her focus as she closed her eyes. With a movie-like visualization, the symbols played out in her mind. As the sun rose, she saw a bird take flight, a path winding through the forest, and a star shining above, guiding the way.

She realized the answer wasn't a word or a phrase, but an action. The star represented a destination, a place she needed to find. It was a guiding light, pointing the way to her next adventure. But where was the star?

Jessica looked around, her eyes scanning the backyard landscape. She considered the symbols again: day, night, journey, and the guiding star. She spotted a bright star-shaped flower blooming amidst the jungle foliage near the crystal grotto. It was a small, delicate blossom, but its vibrant color stood out against the greenery, like a tiny beacon of light.

Excitement bubbled inside her. She had solved the cryptic puzzle that tested both heart and mind! The whispered secrets of the willows had led her to her first genuine trial with hidden stakes, and she had conquered it. This realization filled her with a sense of accomplishment and a greater desire to explore the wonders of her backyard. The solved cryptic puzzle that tested both heart and mind wasn't the answer to a puzzle, but a key to unlocking more adventures within her enchanted kingdom. It was a testament to her ingenuity and the power of observation, proving that even ordinary objects can hold extraordinary secrets if one knows how to look.

The journey to the star-shaped flower was not without its trials. She had to navigate through dense patches of her make-believe jungle, avoiding thorny vines and giant, playful spiders made from twigs and yarn. She had a narrow escape with a "hungry" caterpillar–a green pipe cleaner disguised by her–that threatened to block her path. With determination and clever maneuvering, she overcame every obstacle.

She reached the star-shaped flower, its petals shimmering under the setting sun. Nestled beneath its delicate blossoms, she found a small wooden box, carved with the same symbols as the stone. Inside, nestled on a bed of velvet fabric, was a small, tarnished compass–a true explorer's treasure.

The old compass hummed, showing residual energy. Its needle spun at first, then settled, pointing in a direction she hadn't considered. It pointed towards the far side of the backyard, a section she had never explored—a wild, untamed area beyond her usual play area. This was it—the next chapter in her grand adventure.

The setting sun bathed the backyard in the soft glow of twilight. Jessica, clutching the compass, felt a thrill coursing through her veins. The whispering willows, the hidden river, the solved cryptic puzzle that tested both heart and mind, and the explorer's compass were all coming together, forming a narrative as interesting and exciting as any she had ever read or watched in the nature documentaries that inspired her. This was more than a game; this was a genuine, authentic journey of discovery, right in her backyard. Her backyard, transformed into a magical kingdom of endless possibilities, was ready to reveal its further wonders.

The compass in her hand felt warm, pulsing with a gentle energy that mirrored the excitement bubbling in her chest. The intricate carvings on its surface seemed to shimmer in the twilight, hinting at the mysteries it held. She placed the compass into her miniature backpack, alongside the iridescent blue pebble and a few extra sunflower seeds for Whiskers.

With a deep breath, she turned toward the direction the compass showed. Overgrowth, shadows, and the unknown lay ahead on the path. But Jessica, armed with her imagination, newfound confidence, and trusty explorer's compass, felt a sense of exhilaration and anticipation that only a true adventurer could experience. This journey delved into the uncharted heart of her Backyard Kingdom, offering even more wonders and challenges than she had encountered. She knew this adventure would test her resourcefulness, problem-solving skills, and unwavering spirit. But she was ready. Ready to embark on the next thrilling chapter of her backyard expedition, prepared to face whatever lay hidden in the unexplored reaches of her magical world. Deep down, she knew that Whiskers, her brave companion, would stand by her side.

Chapter 5: The First Riddle and Its Solution

The compass, a tiny, tarnished thing, felt warm in Jessica's hand. It hummed with a faint energy, a subtle vibration that sent a shiver of excitement down her spine. After a moment of frantic spinning, the needle settled, pointing towards the far corner of the backyard, a shadowy area dominated by the old, dilapidated shed. This was unfamiliar territory, unexplored and mysterious. A thrill, sharp and exhilarating, coursed through her.

Jessica approached the shed, its weathered wood groaning under the weight of years and neglect. Cobwebs draped from its eaves like ghostly curtains, and the air hung heavy with the smell of damp earth and decaying leaves. The shed, a place she avoided, now seemed to beckon her with untold secrets.

Jessica spotted a small, smooth stone near the shed's base, half-hidden beneath a tangle of overgrown ivy. This one was different, unlike the stones scattered throughout the backyard. It was a rich brown, polished smooth by time and weather. Upon closer inspection, she noticed a series of tiny carvings etched into its surface, forming a cryptic puzzle that tested both heart and mind.

Someone wrote the cryptic puzzle in a playful rhyme. "Where shadows dance and play, seek near the shed where time stands still; a treasure waits, come what may, hidden near the old wood's chill."

Jessica giggled at the simplicity of the rhyme, yet it held a certain charm. She pondered the clues, her eyes scanning the area around the shed. "Shadows dance and play" likely refers to the way sunlight filtered through the leaves, creating shifting patterns of light and shadow. The phrase "Near the shed where time stands still" creates an image of a timeless place surrounding the shed, while "hidden near the old wood's chill" evokes the shed's own cold, damp environment.

Jessica examined the area, her eyes searching for any hint of the treasure. She peered behind the shed, its weathered wood crumbling in places, revealing glimpses of its interior. Nothing. She searched under the overgrown ivy, lifting aside the thick leaves—still nothing.

Then she noticed a slight, shaped indentation in the earth near the shed's base, almost perfectly concealed by a clump of weeds. She kneeled down and brushed away the weeds, revealing a small, carved wooden box. The artisan crafted it, adorning its surface with delicate floral patterns; its dark, polished brown wood seemed to absorb the surrounding light.

With trembling hands, Jessica lifted the lid of the box. Inside, nestled on a bed of soft, moss-green velvet, lay a single, iridescent feather. It shimmered with an ethereal glow, its colors shifting and changing with every movement. It wasn't gold or jewels, nor was it a pirate's hoard or a king's ransom. Jessica considered it far more valuable.

The feather seemed to pulsate with a gentle light, its colors shifting from deep emerald green to sapphire blue to fiery ruby red. Its weight felt negligible; a breath would lift it. She held it up to the light, admiring its intricate structure, its delicate barbules shimmering like tiny prisms. It felt magical, otherworldly. This wasn't any feather; it felt ancient, imbued with mystery and wonder. The cryptic puzzle that tested both heart and mind centered on unearthing hidden secrets, not riches; it focused on the joy of discovery and unexpected beauty.

As Jessica held the iridescent feather, she realized something else: the clues weren't about finding a specific location; instead, they required cultivating patience, observation, and an adventurous mindset. The treasure wasn't the feather; it was the entire journey, solving the cryptic puzzle that tested both heart and mind, and overcoming a trial with hidden stakes.

Jessica considered the feather far more than a pretty trinket. The badge of honor symbolized her newfound adventure; it served as a reminder that those with keen eyes and adventurous spirits often find extraordinary treasures. It was a testament to the explorer's blossoming sense of adventure, complementing her compass.

The sun began its slow descent, painting the sky in vibrant hues of orange and purple. Jessica's cradled feather glowed more intensely as daylight waned. She placed it in her backpack beside the compass, the sensation a profound sense of accomplishment and anticipation. The feather symbolized her inner strength, growing confidence, and the incredible power of her imagination. She knew the next trial with hidden stakes was waiting for her somewhere in her Backyard Kingdom. A towering mountain, the old oak tree, beckoned her towards its summit.

The journey was not over. She was becoming a true explorer, discovering not only the hidden wonders of her backyard but also the boundless potential of her imagination.

Long, playful shadows stretched across the backyard as the sun set, turning familiar objects into fantastical shapes. The old shed, a source of apprehension, now stood as a landmark of her first successful expedition, symbolizing her growing courage and resilience. The neglected path to the shed now appeared well-worn, showcasing her tenacity and skill in solving the cryptic puzzle that tested both heart and mind. Each step towards the shed was a testament to her adventurous spirit, growing self-reliance, and confidence in her abilities.

As Jessica turned her gaze towards the next potential adventure, she realized that the spirit of exploration was not about reaching the destination, but about embracing the journey itself. It was about the joy of discovery, the thrill of venturing beyond the known, and the personal growth that comes from exploring the unexpected. She smiled, a broad, genuine smile, and turned toward the next phase of her extraordinary backyard journey, ready to face whatever wonders or challenges lay ahead. Her backyard held an unsolved cryptic puzzle that tested both heart and minds, undiscovered treasures, and unexperienced adventures.

Chapter 6: Navigating the Flowerbed Jungle

Still warm in her pocket, the iridescent feather seemed to thrum with a faint energy as Jessica approached the flowerbeds. They weren't ordinary flowerbeds anymore; in her mind, they transformed into a dense, vibrant jungle, a riot of color and life. Towering sunflowers, their faces like golden suns, loomed over her, their petals forming a thick, rustling canopy. The air hummed with the buzz of bumblebees, their fuzzy bodies a blur of motion as they flitted from bloom to bloom. The petunias and roses intensified their familiar scents, creating a heady, intoxicating perfume.

Jessica felt a thrill of excitement course through her. This differed from the shadowed area near the shed. This jungle felt alive, pulsating with energy. She pushed aside a curtain of tall foxgloves, their bell-shaped flowers a delicate purple, and stepped into the heart of the flowerbed jungle.

The ground beneath her feet was soft and yielding, a carpet of moss and fallen petals. The air was thick with the scent of damp earth and blooming flowers. Giant daisies, their petals as large as dinner plates, bobbed in the breeze, creating a hypnotic, swaying motion. Jessica walked through a fantastical dreamscape, vibrant, full of unexpected wonders.

A flash of iridescent wings caught her eye. A butterfly, unlike any she had ever seen, landed on a nearby rosebush. Its wings shimmered with all the rainbow colors, shifting and changing with every movement, like a tiny, fluttering kaleidoscope. As Jessica watched, mesmerized, the butterfly's antennae twitched, and a small, clear, and melodious voice spoke.

"Lost, little explorer?" the butterfly chirped, its voice like tinkling bells.

Jessica gasped. A talking butterfly? This surpassed the extraordinariness of the iridescent feather. "I... I think so," she stammered, still stunned. Remembering the legends her grandmother told her, she added, "I'm trying to find a hidden cave under the porch."

"Ah, the Whispering Cave," the butterfly replied, its voice filled with a tone of knowing. "Many seek its secrets, but few find their way. To reach it, you must follow the path of the hummingbirds."

Jessica looked around, her eyes scanning the flowerbed jungle.

Hummingbirds? She had seen hummingbirds flitting among the flowers, their tiny wings a blur of motion. But how could they guide her to the cave?

"The hummingbirds don't leave a trail of breadcrumbs, child," the butterfly chuckled, a delicate sound like the rustling of leaves. "Only those with keen observation and a listening ear can see their path."

The butterfly then fluttered its iridescent wings, revealing tiny symbols etched into their surface, each with a small, almost invisible design. Jessica squinted, trying to make out the symbols. The sequence showed flowers: a sunflower, a rose, a daisy, a foxglove, and a small bluebell-like flower.

"These are the sentinels," the butterfly explained. "Following the flowers in this order will reveal the path to the Whispering Cave," the butterfly explained.

With a final flutter of its wings, the butterfly soared into the air, disappearing among the swaying flowers. Jessica felt a surge of determination. It was an explorer-worthy adventure! She memorized the sequence of flowers–sunflower, rose, daisy, foxglove, and bluebell–and set off, her heart pounding. The search was hard. The flowerbed jungle was a maze of vibrant blooms, a labyrinth of twisting stems and rustling leaves. Jessica had to navigate the dense foliage, pushing aside leaves and bending under branches, her eyes scanning for the next flower in the sequence.

Finding the sunflower was easy; it was one of the tallest plants in the jungle, its golden face glowing in the afternoon sun. Next came the rose, its deep crimson petals a striking contrast to the surrounding greenery. The daisy, with its delicate white petals, was harder to find, hidden amongst a cluster of other flowers. With its tall spire of purple bells, the foxglove stood out amidst a patch of ferns.

Finding the last flower, the small bluebell, proved the most challenging. Jessica searched high and low, her heart sinking. Just as she was about to give up, she spotted a tiny, delicate bluebell tucked away under a large fern. Although hidden, its vibrant blue color almost revealed it. As she reached the bluebell, the ground beneath her feet seemed to shift. With a gentle click, a hidden passage opened before her, revealing a dark opening leading down into the earth. They had reached the Whispering Cave!

Jessica took a deep breath and stepped into the darkness, clutching the iridescent feather. The feather pulsed with light, illuminating the path before her. A mysterious scent hung in the cool, damp cave air. The hummingbirds' song was fainter here, replaced by a soft, almost imperceptible whisper of the wind.

The adventure was far from over; it had only begun. As she ventured deeper into the cave, her heart pounding with anticipation, she knew that the Whispering Cave held even more secrets, waiting to be uncovered by her intrepid spirit. The path ahead was dark; a cool, mysterious air prevailed; outside sounds were distant. This was the heart of her Backyard Kingdom's magic, and Jessica was ready for whatever marvels or challenges it held.

Chapter 7: The Talking Butterfly and Its Clues

The butterfly, its wings a breathtaking display of shifting rainbows, settled into a dew-kissed petal. Its antennae, delicate as spun gold, twitched as it regarded Jessica with knowing eyes. "The Whispering Cave," it began, its voice a gentle chime, "holds secrets older than the oak tree itself. Many have sought its entrance, but few have succeeded."

Jessica, her heart thrumming with anticipation, leaned closer. "How do I find it?" she whispered, her voice audible above the buzzing of bees and the rustling of leaves.

The butterfly chuckled, a sound like the tinkling of tiny bells. Young explorer, the path remains elusive. "First, you must understand the language of the wind, whispering secrets. Listen, child. The wind carries secrets, whispers of the past, and murmurs of the future. Can you decipher its messages?"

Jessica closed her eyes, focusing on the gentle breeze that rustled through the flowerbed jungle. She listened, trying to discern any patterns, any hidden meanings in the sounds. The whispering of leaves transformed from a cacophony to a rhythmic symphony. A soft swishing from the foxgloves urged closer inspection.

The butterfly's voice broke into her reverie. "The wind speaks in echoes, little one. It reflects the sounds of the past, the secrets held within the earth. Seek where the earth whispers back the wind, whispering secrets's song, where the past's echoes meet the present's murmurs." Jessica pondered this. Echoes of the past... the murmurs of the present... Where could one find such a place? She recalled the stories her grandmother had told, tales of hidden areas, of magic woven into the fabric of her backyard. Could the entrance to the cave somehow reflect those stories? Perhaps familiar and fantastical elements could merge there?

"The cave guardians are not unkind," the butterfly continued, sensing Jessica's confusion. But they keep a close watch.

The butterfly then revealed a cryptic puzzle that tested both heart and mind, etched into its iridescent wings, visible to the naked eye. Jessica squinted, straining to decipher the cryptic symbols. The first cryptic puzzle revealed when the butterfly shifted its left forewing, was a simple picture: a sunflower leaning towards a rock. Jessica pondered this for a moment. Reaching for the sun, the sunflower might show a sunny spot. The solid, unyielding rock could hint at something sturdy, perhaps a stone wall or a part of the house's foundation.

The second cryptic puzzle on the right hind wing depicted a winding path to a small, shadowed area. This suggested a hidden route, perhaps a trail obscured by vegetation or camouflaged. This aligned with the butterfly's warning of the cave hidden in plain sight.

The final cryptic puzzle, a delicate image on the butterfly's left hind wing, showed a small, glowing crystal nestled within a cluster of ivy. This suggested a connection to the glowing crystals Jessica had glimpsed under the porch, a hint that the cave might contain similar luminous formations.

"These are not puzzles, little explorer," the butterfly explained. "They are keys, each unlocking a layer of the mystery.

Follow the clues, trust your instincts, and you will reveal the entrance to the Whispering Cave. With a final flutter of its magnificent wings, the butterfly soared into the air, its shimmering form disappearing amongst the swaying flowers. Jessica took a deep breath. The cryptic puzzle was a trial with hidden stakes, but she felt a surge of excitement. This was more than a game; it was a true quest, a journey into the heart of her backyard's magic.

She began her search, her eyes scanning the flower beds with renewed focus. She looked for the sunflower leaning towards a rock, the winding path, and the ivy-covered area that might conceal a glowing crystal. The flowerbed jungle, a vibrant maze, now held clues she could not spot moments earlier. She noticed a sunflower almost hidden amidst the ivy, its stalk leaning toward a section of the porch's foundation.

Following the sunflower's lead, she spotted a small, overgrown path concealed by tall foxgloves. Its winding course led to a darker region under the porch.

Jessica followed the path, her heart pounding with a mix of excitement and apprehension. The air grew cooler as she neared the shadowed area, a sense of mystery enveloping her. She pushed aside thick ivy and uncovered a tiny, glowing crystal nestled within the leaves, radiating a soft, ethereal light. The crystal seemed to pulse, almost as if responding to her presence.

As she reached out to touch the crystal, she heard a subtle click, a faint sound almost lost in the background noise of the jungle. The earth beneath her feet shifted, and a section of the porch's base moved inwards, revealing a dark, inviting opening–the entrance to the Whispering Cave. She had solved the butterfly's cryptic puzzle. Jessica felt a wave of triumph wash over her, a sense of accomplishment that fueled her desire to step into the unknown.

Chapter 8: Discovering the Crystal Cave

With a deep breath, Jessica squeezed through the narrow opening, the cool, damp air washing over her like a refreshing wave. The entrance was small, wider than her shoulders, but it opened into a spacious cavern. The air hummed with a low, resonant thrum, a vibration deep within her chest. It wasn't unpleasant; instead, it felt invigorating, a subtle energy that seemed to pulse with the earth.

Her eyes adjusted to the dim light, revealing a spectacle of breathtaking beauty. The cave walls displayed countless glittering crystals, resembling a million captured stars. They were not the dull, gray crystals she sometimes found in rock shops; these were vibrant, alive with an inner light that shimmered with every hue imaginable. Amethysts pulsed with a deep violet glow, emeralds blazed with a verdant fire, and diamonds sparkled with an almost blinding brilliance. Crystals varied in size, from pebble-sized to her head-sized, creating a dazzling mixture of shapes and colors.

A path, illuminated by the crystals' light, wound deeper into the earth, vanishing into the shadows. The air cooled, and the earth's hum intensified with each step. She ran her hand along a giant amethyst crystal, the sensation tingling as her fingers brushed its surface—a gentle warmth pulsed from the crystal, responding to her touch.

As she ventured deeper, the cave opened into a larger chamber.

Here, the crystals formed intricate formations, some resembling towering spires, while others resembled delicate light curtains. A massive geode pulsed with a soft, ethereal glow at the center of the chamber. It was larger than anything she had ever seen — a breathtaking, translucent crystal sphere filled with a swirling nebula of light and color. It seemed to hum with a silent energy, a powerful, almost palpable force.

Jessica approached the geode, sensing a sense of awe and wonder. She reached out a hand, her fingers brushing the cool, smooth surface. The geode responded with a gentle warmth, a comforting energy that seemed to soothe her anxieties. It was as if the geode were whispering secrets, revealing truths hidden within her heart.

As she stood there, lost in contemplation, a small, glittering creature emerged behind one of the crystal spires. It resembled a tiny dragon, no bigger than her thumb, with scales that shimmered with all the rainbow colors. Its wings, delicate as butterfly wings, beat, creating a soft, tinkling sound. The tiny dragon regarded her with intelligent, curious eyes.

"Welcome, little explorer," it chirped, its voice a delicate tone. You have found the heart of the Whispering Cave." Jessica gasped, surprised by the creature's ability to speak. "You...you can talk?" The dragon chuckled, a sound like the tinkling of tiny bells. "Of course, I can talk. All creatures in this cave possess a certain... eloquence. We are the guardians of this place, protectors of its secrets."

"Secrets?" Jessica asked, her curiosity piqued.

"Indeed," the dragon replied. "The crystals hold the echoes of the past, the whispers of the earth. They contain stories untold, knowledge long forgotten. But only those with pure hearts and open minds can understand their language."

The dragon then led Jessica deeper into the cave, revealing hidden chambers filled with even more wondrous crystal formations. In one chamber, the crystals formed intricate patterns that resembled constellations, mapping the stars like ancient watchers in the night sky. In another, the crystals created a shimmering waterfall, cascading down the cave walls in a breathtaking display of light and motion. Along the way, the dragon shared tales of ancient civilizations that once sought refuge within its depths, of magical creatures that lived among the crystals, and of powerful energies that flowed through the earth. Jessica listened, her imagination running wild as she envisioned the scenes unfolding before her.

As they explored, Jessica noticed the crystals seemed to respond to her emotions. When she felt happy, the crystals glowed with a brighter light. When she felt sad, the light dimmed. It was as if the crystals mirrored her inner state, reflecting her sensations. The dragon explained the crystals were sentient beings, capable of sensing and responding to emotions. They were not mere rocks, but living beings, imbued with a mystical energy that connected them to the earth and all other living things. This cave was like a living heart.

Jessica spent hours exploring the cave with the tiny dragon, learning about its history, magic, and secrets. The cave evoked within her an unprecedented sense of connection and belonging. Jessica felt a bond with the cave; the sunset, with shadows lengthening at the entrance, signaled her departure. The dragon led her back to the entrance, its small form shimmering in the fading light.

"Thank you," Jessica whispered. "This has been the most amazing experience."

"The cave will always be here," the dragon replied, its voice gentle but firm. "Whenever you need to reconnect with yourself, nature, or the magic that lies within, you can always return." With a final flutter of its wings, the dragon disappeared into the cave's shadows, leaving Jessica alone in the twilight. She emerged from the cave, blinking in the fading light. The adventure exceeded her expectations; it proved to be fulfilling. The crystal cave held a magic that resonated deep within her soul.

The extraordinary realm, created from an ordinary backyard, revealed that adventure, magic, and wonder exist in the most unexpected places. Her gaze upon the small opening confirmed this was the beginning. The whispering willows along the make-believe river beckoned, whispering of further mysteries and hidden pathways waiting to be uncovered in her magical backyard.

Chapter 9: The Cave Guardians and Their Test

The path, illuminated by the ethereal glow of the crystals, continued its winding descent. Moving deeper into the earth, Jessica felt a noticeable chill in the air, dampness clinging to her skin. A vibrant hum, intensifying to a deep thrum, vibrated her chest and bones. In rhythm with the subterranean heartbeat, the crystals pulsed, their light flickering and shifting in a mesmerizing dance.

A vast cavern, larger than the one she'd left, opened before her. Towering spires and cascading formations did not fill this chamber, unlike the previous space. The water wasn't still; it rippled, reflecting the light of the crystals in a kaleidoscope of colors. And within this luminous pool, countless tiny creatures floated, their bodies emitting a soft, pulsating light.

They were like fireflies. Their bodies were not the familiar pale yellow of common fireflies, but glowed with a spectrum of colors — shimmering blues, vibrant greens, and delicate pinks and purples. And instead of the typical flickering light, their glow was steady and unwavering, as if each tiny creature held a miniature star within its translucent body. Their wings, however, were unlike anything she'd ever seen. They were gossamer-thin, almost invisible, spun from moonlight, shimmering and iridescent in the underwater light.

As she watched, captivated, one of the luminous creatures drifted closer, its light illuminating the surrounding water with an enchanting glow. It stopped in front of Jessica, its tiny, multifaceted eyes gazing into her soul. A sound like little bells followed.

"Welcome, traveler," it said. "We are the Guardians of the Whispering Cave. We protect the secrets held within these walls, guarding the knowledge and wisdom of the earth."

Jessica gasped, speechless. She'd encountered the talking dragon, but these... these were something else. They were smaller, more delicate, their presence more ethereal. "We have been watching you," another Guardian chimed in, its voice melodious. "We sense a pure heart and a curious mind. But you must prove your worthiness to delve deeper into the cave's secrets." Jessica's heart pounded in her chest. A test? What kind of test?

"The test is simple," a third Guardian explained. "It is a test of kindness and observation. Look around you, child. Observe the world beneath the earth, and let your heart guide you."

Jessica looked around the cavern. The shimmering pool teemed with luminous creatures, each unique in its coloring and the intensity of its light. She noticed some Guardians clustered together in small groups, while others floated alone. Some seemed to prefer the shallower areas near the pool's edge, while others remained deep within the water's heart. The patterns of their movements were fluid and graceful, a silent dance of light and energy.

Then she noticed something else. Nestled amongst the luminous creatures, a small, dark object lay on the bottom of the pool. It looked like a pebble, but something about it made her pause. She saw a slight, almost imperceptible movement that seemed to pulsate. As she watched, she realized it was a tiny, injured firefly, its light dimmed and flickering. A small, sharp crystal shard trapped it, preventing it from freeing itself.

Without hesitation, Jessica entered the pool, the cool water shocking her hand. She lifted the shard, freeing the tiny firefly. Freeing it from its constraints intensified the creature's glow. The Guardians watched her every move, their luminous bodies pulsating. Once Jessica released the firefly, allowing it to swim away and rejoin the others, the surrounding air seemed to shimmer.

"You have passed the test," one guardian declared, its voice filled with approval. Your observant eye and kindness reveal the purity of your heart. These celebrate natural world preservation. You, little explorer, have proven yourself worthy."

Every Guardian illuminated the cavern's far end. An unseen passage, hidden behind a curtain of shimmering crystals, now shone. The crystals seemed to part, revealing a path leading further into the earth.

"This path leads to the Heart of the Cave," the first Guardian announced. "There, you will find the knowledge you seek." Feeling excited and grateful, Jessica thanked the Guardians for their test and for guiding her. She stepped through the revealed passage, the luminous creatures forming a glowing escort for her as she ventured deeper into the cave's mysterious heart. As she took each step, the air grew warmer, and the humming transformed into a melodic song. Intensifying, the light illuminated new wonders around her. With an inner light causing them to glow, the crystals seemed to beckon her closer, their welcoming energy pulling her forward.

The opening passage revealed a vast cavern, surpassing in grandeur even its former glory. Lost in shadow, the ceiling, high and domed, ascended into an abyss of darkness. Lining the walls were enormous crystals, every single one emitting its own distinct and mesmerizing color and an intensity of light unlike any other. Jessica felt the strangely warm sand beneath her feet, the soft, glowing grains covering the entire floor. A giant geode stood in the center of the chamber, bathed in the ethereal glow of the surrounding crystals. It was unlike anything she had ever seen before. It was perfectly spherical, translucent, and immense, at least ten feet in diameter. Inside, swirling colors and patterns of light shifted and changed, creating a mesmerizing spectacle.

As Jessica approached the geode, she saw intricate carvings covering the cavern walls. They depicted scenes of ancient beings interacting with the crystals, communicating with them through touch and gestures. Some figures appeared to be harnessing the energy of the crystals, while others seemed to learn from them, their expressions reflecting a deep sense of awe and wonder.

She touched the carving and felt a strange energy emanating from it. It was as if the stones whispered stories into her mind, revealing glimpses of ancient knowledge and forgotten wisdom. The carvings depicted the history of this hidden world, its above-ground connections, and its deep-seated earthly origins.

The geode in the cavern's center pulsed with light, its inner brilliance intensifying and dimming in rhythm with the earth's humming. It was like a living, breathing heart, radiating energy and warmth. Jessica stood before it, awestruck by its beauty and power. A profound connection to this place, its crystals, and its ancient inhabitants filled her.

The Guardians floated around her, their luminous bodies creating a soft, ethereal glow. Although they were silent, their presence felt comforting and reassuring. Jessica's journey and the cave itself were under their protection. They watched silently as she explored the cavern, sensing the connection to the energy of the crystals, the ancient history, and the earth itself.

Jessica spent hours exploring the cavern, her imagination soaring as she deciphered the carvings and understood the stories the crystals held within. She learned of the ancient civilizations that sought refuge here, the magical beings that had lived amongst the crystals, and the powerful energies that flowed through the earth. She uncovered humanity and nature once coexisted, recognizing their interdependence. It was a message of balance, sustainability, and respect for the power of nature — a message that resonated within her heart. The experience altered her perspective, causing her to appreciate the importance of protecting the environment and preserving the world's natural wonders. Her ordinary backyard transformed: boundless wonder, endless potential. And as the light faded, signaling the end of her magical journey, she knew that a part of this incredible, secret world would always remain within her heart.

Chapter 10: The Crystal Heart and Its Power

With ever-increasing intensity, light shimmered on the walls. The humming grew louder, resonating deep within Jessica's chest, a powerful, rhythmic pulse that seemed to echo the beat of her own heart. The air grew warmer, carrying the scent of something sweet and earthy, like wildflowers blooming in the spring. Ahead, the passage opened into a breathtaking view.

It was a vast, circular cavern, its ceiling lost in the shadows far above. Towering crystals, taller than any Jessica had seen, lined the walls, their surfaces reflecting the light in a dazzling display of color. The crystals weren't inanimate objects; they pulsed with a soft, internal light, their hues shifting and changing in a mesmerizing dance of light and shadow. Some were a deep sapphire blue, others a vibrant emerald green, and others shimmered with amethyst purple and fiery orange. The sheer variety and intensity of the light were overwhelming.

This cavern's centerpiece outshone its crystals. It was a colossal geode, a spherical crystal formation at least ten feet in diameter. It pulsed with a gentle, rhythmic beat, its translucent shell revealing an inner world of swirling colors and light. The light within the geode wasn't static; it flowed and shifted, creating patterns that seemed to tell a story, a silent symphony of light and energy. The colors were stunning, swirling, and blending in a mesmerizing dance as deep reds and oranges gave way to vivid greens and blues.

Jessica felt an immediate connection to it, filled with awe and wonder. As she drew closer, the humming intensified, becoming a vibrant song that filled the cavern. The air around the geode radiated warmth, a comforting embrace that eased any lingering apprehension. A powerful heartbeat resonated from the earth's core, the geode's light a pulsating reflection. Jessica reached out a hand, hesitant but drawn to the warmth radiating from its surface. As her fingers brushed against the smooth, cool crystal, a jolt of energy surged through her, a wave of power invigorated her from head to toe.

The Guardians, still accompanying her, formed a ring around the geode, their luminous bodies echoing the colors within. They didn't speak, but their presence was comforting, a silent affirmation of her journey. Jessica felt a profound sense of peace and connection, as if she were part of something larger than herself, ancient and powerful. She understood, at that moment, the significance of the Crystal Heart. It wasn't a beautiful geode, but a symbol of the power of imagination — a tangible representation of the magic within her heart and the world around her. The extraordinary adventures found in even the most unexpected places, including her backyard, testified to its significance.

The pulsating light of the Crystal Heart illuminated the elaborate carvings on the cavern walls, and she studied them for a long time. These carvings were more detailed than those she had seen earlier, depicting scenes of ancient civilizations interacting with the crystals, harnessing their energy, and learning from their wisdom. The scenes were vivid, filled with movement and emotion. Jessica experienced a forgotten history, an untold story spanning centuries. She saw people working in harmony with nature, respecting its rhythms, and living in harmony with the earth. They were learning from the crystals, understanding their power and potential to heal and inspire.

Observing the carvings, she uncovered the profound connection between the crystals and the earth, how they pulsed in sync with the planet's energy, resonating with its heartbeat. The message highlighted interdependence within nature. The Crystal Heart wasn't a beautiful object; it was a living entity, a source of energy and wisdom, a symbol of the power of nature and the importance of respecting and preserving it.

The humming intensified again; the geode pulsating with greater vigor, the light within shifted and changed, creating a dazzling display of color. Jessica felt warmth spreading through her body, and she experienced an increase in energy and well-being. The Crystal Heart seemed to communicate with her, sharing its wisdom and power. She felt a surge of inspiration, a renewed sense of purpose. Her journey wasn't about exploring her backyard but discovering her potential, inner strength, and resilience. The Crystal Heart was a reminder of her ability to create, imagine, and believe in herself.

With a newfound clarity, she understood the guardians' test. Kindness wasn't the issue; It was about seeing the magic in the everyday, the wonder in the ordinary. The core of it was the belief in her imagination's power and the boundless possibilities it offered. The Crystal Heart, therefore, wasn't a trophy; it symbolized this journey, a reminder of her capacity to find wonder and magic everywhere she looked. It was a beacon of self-belief, a tangible manifestation of the power of imagination and the beauty of believing in oneself.

Jessica knew she couldn't take the Crystal Heart with her. This magical place's heart connected the cavern, the earth, and her amazing backyard. But she carried its message within her: a profound understanding of the power of nature, the interconnectedness of all living things, and the enduring strength of her imagination. The experience had broadened her perspective, and awakened a deeper appreciation for the wonders of the natural world and the magic that lives within herself. As the light faded, signaling the end of her incredible journey, she thanked the Guardians for their guidance and protection. Their luminous bodies pulsed, a silent farewell.

Jessica stepped back from the Crystal Heart, feeling a profound sense of gratitude and accomplishment. She carried the memory of the Crystal Heart and the lessons it taught her, not as a physical object, but as a powerful inner light — a reminder of her potential and ability to create magic in her own life. She knew this magical adventure had only begun; the whispers of the jungle and the cave's secrets would continue to guide her on future journeys of self-discovery. The ordinary backyard, forever transformed in her eyes, held the promise of countless more adventures yet to come. Following the Crystal Heart's light, she returned to the familiar, now wondrous, upper world. She felt quiet joy and deep contentment on her journey back. She knew that the magic she had experienced would stay with her always, a constant reminder of the power of her imagination and the boundless adventures that awaited her in the ordinary world, now forever infused with extraordinary possibilities.

Chapter 11: Scaling the Oak Tree Mountain

The air grew cooler as Jessica started her ascent of the Oak Tree Mountain. Whiskers, her adventurous hamster, clung to the strap of her backpack, his tiny claws digging into the fabric. Below, the Crystal Cavern receded, its shimmering light fading into the distance, a memory already etched into the fabric of her being. The base of the oak tree, now a formidable mountain in her imaginative landscape, was a jumble of roots, thick as pythons, that snaked across the ground like ancient, slumbering serpents.

Jessica chose a sturdy root, its bark rough beneath her hand, and pulled herself up. The beginning proved challenging. She felt a thrill of excitement mixed with a healthy dose of apprehension. This was the ultimate trial with hidden stakes, the ultimate test of her courage and climbing skills. The wind whispered secrets through the leaves, high above, a chorus of encouragement and a reminder of the magnitude of her undertaking.

She gripped a thick branch, its smooth bark against her palms, and hauled herself upwards. The climb was more challenging than she had expected. Placed branches were not always available. Other times, she had to maneuver around obstacles—knots in the branches, gaps between them—testing her agility and balance. But with each successful maneuver, her confidence grew. Despite underlying apprehension, exhilaration and triumphant joy predominated.

Whiskers, ever the brave companion, peeked out from his perch in the backpack, his tiny whiskers twitching. Jessica smiled down at him, offering a word of encouragement. "Almost there, Whiskers," she whispered, her voice audible above the rustling leaves. He chirped in response, a tiny squeak of encouragement that warmed her heart. He was her steadfast companion.

As she climbed higher, the view became more spectacular. Below her, a fantastical landscape unfolded in her imagination, the backyard transformed into a vibrant tapestry of enchanting details. The swing set, now a formidable pirate ship, bobbed in the breeze; the flowerbeds, transformed into a dense jungle, teemed with life, their colorful blooms shining like precious jewels. She could see her house nestled amongst the trees, a cozy haven in this fantastical world she had created. A testament to boundless imagination, it was a world of wonder.

Moments of both physical trials with hidden stakes and profound beauty punctuated the climb. She'd pause, clinging to a branch, to marvel at the intricate patterns of the bark, the delicate veins of the leaves, the way the sunlight filtered through the canopy, creating dancing patterns of light and shadow on the forest floor. It was a meditative experience, a chance to connect with the nature around her and appreciate its beauty and resilience. Life filled the world above;

The higher she climbed, the stronger the wind. Whispering secrets became buffeting her as she struggled upward. She had to concentrate, focus on each handhold and foothold, and ensure her grip was secure before moving on. Several times, she slipped, her heart pounding in her chest, but she recovered, her reflexes honed by the challenges she had already overcome.

Finally, she topped the mountain. She emerged onto a broad, flat area at the top of the oak tree, a clearing bathed in sunlight. It was breathtaking. The view was panoramic, encompassing her entire backyard and beyond. The ordinary world stretched out before her, transformed by the lens of her imagination into a landscape of breathtaking beauty and adventure.

She sat down; her legs trembling from the exertion, and took a deep breath, savoring the moment. Whiskers emerged from the backpack, stretching and yawning, as exhausted and exhilarated as she was. From this vantage point, she could see everything: the sparkling river, the whispering willows, the cave entrance hidden beneath the porch, and the distant hills, painted in the hues of the setting sun. This sight, a reminder of extraordinary adventures in ordinary places, would forever remain etched in her memory.

She pulled out her journal and wrote, recording her ascent, observations, and sensations. The words flowed, as if guided by an unseen hand, capturing the essence of her extraordinary journey. She wrote about the challenges she had overcome, the beauty she had witnessed, and the sense of accomplishment that filled her heart. Whiskers, her devoted companion, provided comfort and quiet support, a detail she documented.

As the sun set, casting a warm, golden glow over the landscape, she felt a profound sense of peace. She had scaled Oak Tree Mountain, conquered her fears, and uncovered a deeper connection with nature and herself. The ordinary backyard had revealed its extraordinary secrets, the boundless possibilities of imagination, resilience, and the remarkable power of belief in oneself. The adventure wasn't over; it had only begun. The golden sunset cast a shimmering light on the world below, brimming with untold adventures, showcasing the magic within her and her world. The descent was much easier, her confidence soaring after her triumphant ascent. She slid down branches, her laughter echoing through the trees, whiskers clinging to her backpack, a tiny, furry shadow in the deepening twilight.

Landing, she felt grateful. The memory of the climb, the view from the summit, and the quiet satisfaction of achievement would forever remain with her, a cherished part of her childhood memories. Gazing at the towering oak tree, now resembling a grand mountain, she realized magic remained within rustling leaves, whispering winds, and her vast imagination.

Chapter 12: The View from the Summit

The summit was flat, a small, sun-drenched plateau at the crown of Oak Tree Mountain. Jessica gasped. Height held less appeal than the mental transformation of the landscape viewed from above. From below, the backyard had felt vast, a sprawling wilderness to be conquered. From above, it felt... intimate. Familiar, yet new.

From the ground, the pirate ship swing set resembled a mighty galleon; now, it's a miniature vessel in a green sea. The flowerbed jungle, a dense and somewhat daunting thicket, had now become a vibrant mosaic, with each bloom a tiny jewel sparkling in the sunlight. She could even make out the individual petals of the sunflowers, their faces tilted towards the sun like friendly giants.

The Crystal Cavern, her first major expedition, was a tiny glint of light, a shimmering secret tucked beneath the porch, a testament to the adventures already accomplished. The make-believe river, carved from the winding path between the rose bushes, snaked its way through the landscape like a silver ribbon, disappearing into the distance.

From this height, Jessica saw connections she hadn't noticed before. Across the lawn, the shifting shadows of towering maple trees created intricate patterns that changed with the sun's movement. The color of the grass ranged from emerald green in the open to golden hues in sunny patches, deepening to darker shades where the shadows fell. Each branching pattern silhouetted against the sky formed a unique and intricate design.

She noticed a tiny hummingbird hovering near the trumpet vine, its wings a blur of motion, its body a jewel of iridescent green and ruby red. From below, it would have been a flash of color, missed. But from above, she could appreciate its grace, beauty, and effortless flight. Even tiny creatures held significant roles within their complex ecosystem.

A family of squirrels scampering across the oak tree's branches, chattering in a language she couldn't understand but somehow felt. Their playful movements and acrobatic leaps made her smile. She had almost missed them during her ascent, too focused on the climb to notice the more minor details.

Looking further afield, beyond the confines of her backyard kingdom, she saw the rooftops of her neighbors' houses, each with a unique architectural statement against the backdrop of the summer sky. She could make out Mrs. Rodriguez's bright red geraniums spilling over her window box, a splash of color in the otherwise muted tones of the neighborhood. Mr. Lee's manicured lawn, a testament to his dedication and care, extended as far as the eye could see.

The distance gave her a new perspective on her community, making her realize how interconnected everything was and how her backyard adventures were but a small part of a larger, vibrant whole. She viewed the world differently, finding beauty in the commonplace. The afternoon sun's reflection in the distant town lake reminded her of the larger world to which her backyard kingdom belonged.

Jessica pulled out her sketchbook and a pencil, a sense of awe and inspiration washing over her. Unable to capture the scene's essence, she sketched the landscape's outline, the miniature pirate ship, the winding river, and the glittering cave. She filled the page with quick strokes, capturing the essence of the moment, its height, vastness, and intimacy.

A few lines and marks, minor suggestions, conveyed her vision. Whiskers, perched on her shoulder, sniffed at her sketchbook, his tiny nose twitching. He seemed to sense her exhilaration, her deep connection with the world around her. She scratched him behind the ears, feeling his soft fur against her fingers.

As she sat there, drawing and reflecting, the sun dipped below the horizon. The sky exploded with color—bursts of orange, pink, and purple—painting a masterpiece across the canvas of the heavens. The fading light bathed the landscape below in a warm golden glow, transforming and enhancing each element. Even the ordinary seemed extraordinary in the golden hour. The view was breathtaking, a sight she knew she would never forget. Even the most familiar surroundings held untold mysteries, waiting to be uncovered.

Her heart swelled with gratitude and a deep sense of peace. She had not climbed a mountain; she had climbed into a deeper understanding of herself and her world. The triumphant exhilaration of achievement and the quiet satisfaction of having explored her inner and outer landscape had replaced the challenges of the ascent.

She closed her sketchbook, a smile playing on her lips. The descent was much easier; her legs were strong and confident. She slid down the larger branches, pausing only to admire the changing colors of the sky, the way the setting sun painted the clouds in shades of fiery orange and soft rose. Whiskers, ever watchful, remained snug in her backpack.

Reaching the bottom, she found her mother and grandmother waiting, their faces lit up with smiles and a mixture of relief and pride. They had been watching from a distance, marveling at her courage and determination. recounted the breathtaking view from the summit, the playful squirrels, the tiny hummingbird, and the shimmering vista of the nearby town.

They listened, their eyes shining with joy and wonder reflected in her story. It wasn't a story about climbing a tree but of courage, resilience, and the boundless power of imagination. The tale showcased everyday miracles and unforeseen adventures.

That evening, as she shared a meal with her family, Jessica knew her adventure wasn't over. The magic remained, waiting to be rediscovered. The Oak Tree Mountain, her imaginary kingdom, was still there, awaiting her return. Beyond her backyard, the vast world beckoned with many adventures, each as thrilling and fulfilling as the previous. She knew that view from the summit would always remind her of her boundless imagination, adventurous spirit, and the beauty found in her backyard. The world, she realized, was full of mountains waiting to be climbed, and adventures waiting to be uncovered. Only imagination and courage were necessary.

Chapter 13: Encountering the Wind Spirits

The sun warmed Jessica's face as she finished her sketch, the last rays of the setting sun painting the sky in vibrant hues of orange and purple. A gentle breeze rustled through the oak tree's leaves, carrying with it the scents of cut grass and blooming honeysuckle. A playful gust of wind swirled around her feet, lifting a few fallen leaves into a miniature whirlwind. Jessica giggled, a light, joyful sound that echoed in the evening's stillness.

The whirlwind intensified, growing larger and more defined, taking on a whimsical shape that resembled a tiny, dancing creature. More leaves spiraled, forming a small, mischievous figure. Jessica watched, mesmerized, as the leafy creature twirled and spun, its movements graceful and unpredictable.

Then, another gust of wind appeared, forming a second creature, this one larger and more boisterous. It seemed to chase the first, nipping at its leafy heels as they danced across the mountaintop. Many distinct wind spirits emerged, varying in size and strength. Their shifting and changing forms comprised swirling leaves, dancing gusts of wind, and snatches of sunlight.

Jessica felt a surge of exhilaration. Wind spirits, creatures of myth and legend, originated from the breath of mountains and the warmth of the sun. They were playful and captivating. They seemed to sense her presence, their playful dance intensifying as they surrounded her, their leafy forms brushing against her clothes. One of the larger wind spirits, a swirling vortex of bright green leaves, extended a gust of wind towards her, beckoning her to join their dance. Emboldened by their playful energy, Jessica reached out a hand, her fingers tingling as the wind, whispering secrets, enveloped them. The wind spirit tugged at her, swirling her around in a gentle, exhilarating waltz.

The wind spirits' game was one of balance and agility. They tested her limits, pushing and pulling her with playful gusts of wind, challenging her to maintain her footing on the uneven surface of the mountaintop. Jessica laughed, her heart filled with joy and excitement. This game thrilled far beyond the ordinary. She felt at one with nature, her body moving to the wind, whispering secrets' whimsical tune.

Sometimes, the wind, whispering secret spirits, would create a sudden, forceful gust, trying to knock her off balance. Jessica would laugh and brace herself, her feet planted on the ground, her body reacting to maintain her equilibrium. Other times, they would create a gentle breeze that lifted her hair and clothes, caressing her skin with lightness and freedom. She felt as though she were flying, her body soaring with the wind, whispering secrets.

One mischievous wind spirit, a swirling vortex of brown and gold leaves, created a miniature tornado that lifted Jessica's sketchbook. The sketchbook spun gracefully, its pages fluttering like the wings of a giant butterfly before resting at the feet of another wind spirit, a delicate being made of shimmering silver leaves.

Jessica watched, giggling, as the wind, whispering the secret spirit, retrieved the sketchbook and placed it on a nearby rock. Despite its ethereal nature, the wind, whispering secret spirit movements, was precise and gentle. The wind spirits seemed to understand her love for art, respecting her creation even as they teased her. The wind spirits' dance slowed as the sun dipped below the horizon, casting long shadows across the mountaintop. As the light dimmed, their movements became less boisterous, more graceful, their forms fading. Their playfulness, however, never diminished; their interactions remained as delightful as before.

One by one, the wind, whispering secret spirits, faded, their leafy forms dissolving into the darkening twilight, leaving only the gentle whisper of the evening breeze in their wake. The last thing to disappear was the large green wind spirit, which gave Jessica a final, playful nudge before vanishing into the mountain air. Jessica felt a twinge of sadness as the wind, whispering secret spirits, vanished, a poignant reminder of the ephemeral nature of magic and imagination. Yet, the experience filled her with a deep sense of gratitude and joy. She experienced a whimsical encounter with creatures of myth, a memory forever etched in her mind.

The wind spirits' game not only tested her physical limits but, more significantly, challenged her courage and resilience. The game strengthened her belief in the power of imagination and magic in unexpected places. Adventure, she learned from the experience, wasn't about conquering obstacles but embracing life's playful aspects.

As the darkness deepened, Jessica began her descent, the wind whispering secret spirits' laughter still echoing in her ears. She felt a newfound confidence and lightness, a sense of exhilaration that wasn't physical, but spiritual. She felt a genuine connection to nature, the mountain, and its magic.

The easy descent was a testament to his unwavering confidence. Pausing, she gazed at the night sky, its twinkling stars resembling distant jewels set against the dark expanse of space. Moonlight transformed her backyard into a breathtaking, alien landscape. Reaching the bottom, she felt a surge of relief and accomplishment. She had not only climbed Oak Tree Mountain but also encountered its playful guardians, the wind, and whispering secret spirits. She would never forget this adventure, proving the boundless power of imagination and the extraordinary wonders hidden in the most ordinary places.

Her mother and grandmother listened, their eyes wide with amazement and delight at her fantastic tale. They accepted the wind, whispering secret spirits' existence, recognizing the tale's more profound truth.

Jessica felt a deep contentment and peace that evening. More adventure awaited her. The Oak Tree Mountain still held many untold mysteries, many more adventures waiting to unfold. And beyond her backyard, the wider world stretched before her, promising countless other discoveries, each as exciting and rewarding as the last. The encounter with the wind, whispering secret spirits, had only strengthened her determination to explore, discover, and embrace the magic surrounding her. She believed anything was achievable. Mountains beckoned, adventures awaited, and the world brimming with undiscovered marvels. And she was ready for them all.

Chapter 14: The Message in the Wind

As the last of the wind, whispering secret spirits dissolved into the twilight, a single leaf, detached from a nearby willow, fluttered down, landing at Jessica's feet. It wasn't any leaf; it shimmered with an ethereal glow; the veins etched with symbols that seemed to pulse with a faint inner light. Jessica picked up the leaf, her fingers tracing the delicate lines. The symbols weren't letters from any alphabet she recognized, but they felt familiar, resonating deep within her, like a forgotten melody rediscovered. Flipping the leaf, she found a scripted cryptic puzzle that tested both heart and mind on its back.

"Where the old well whispers secrets to the moon, a hidden path awaits, beneath the silent noon. Find the three-chime stone; adventure awaits."

A thrill shot through Jessica. This wasn't a leaf; it was a message, a clue, a promise of further adventure. In their playful departure, the wind, whispering secret spirits, had left her a treasure map, a cryptic invitation to explore yet another hidden corner of her fantastical backyard. The old well! She remembered the well, tucked away behind the overgrown bushes near the edge of her property. It was a relic from a long past, its stone walls covered in moss and ivy, its water stagnant and still. She had never paid much attention to it, viewing it as another old, forgotten landscape feature. But now, thanks to the wind, whispering secret spirit's message, it promised a new adventure.

The puzzle, taxing both intellect and spirit, revealed a hidden path leading to the old well. The "silent noon" intrigued her. Did it mean midday? Or was it a metaphorical phrase hinting at something more mysterious? The "stone with the three whispering chimes" was enigmatic. What kind of stone? And what were the whispering chimes? Were they actual chimes or something more metaphorical, perhaps a sound the wind, whispering secrets made as it passed through a specific arrangement of trees or rocks? The possibilities were endless, each one more exciting than the last.

Jessica's imagination took flight, weaving visions of winding paths cutting through dense thickets and leading to hidden grottos or enchanted caves. Maybe she would stumble upon another group of wind spirits or discover an entirely new realm of fantastical creatures. The possibilities thrilled her, filling her with excitement and a renewed sense of purpose.

The next morning, armed with her sketchbook, a magnifying glass, and a small trowel, Jessica set off on her new quest. Dense and tangled undergrowth made the path to the old well, overgrown and treacherous. But Jessica, fueled by her adventurous spirit, navigated the obstacles, her movements as agile and surefooted as the wind, whispering secret spirits she had encountered the previous evening.

She pushed the bushes and vines aside, revealing the old well in its mossy glory. The weathered and worn stonework stood as a silent sentinel, witnessing countless seasons. The still water in the well, a dark mirror, reflected the sky.

Jessica reread the cryptic puzzle that tested both heart and mind, focusing on the clues she had received. "Where the old well whispers secrets to the moon..." she murmured. She looked around, searching for signs of a hidden path. Then she examined the well's stonework, running her fingers over the rough texture.

It was then that she noticed something peculiar. A visible crack marred the stonework behind the overgrown well. The tiny path, though insignificant, held a connection to the puzzle. She cleared away the brambles, revealing a narrow opening wide enough to squeeze through.

As she looked, she found three small, oddly shaped stones nestled within the crack in the rock. They each emitted a soft, almost imperceptible chime as she touched them. It was like the gentle tinkle of tiny bells — a sound audible yet somehow resonant. They were indeed the three whispering chimes.

With a surge of excitement, Jessica slipped through the opening. The passage was narrow and dark, but she was undeterred. She continued, her curiosity and sense of adventure overriding any initial hesitation. The air grew cooler as she moved deeper, and she could hear the faint sound of running water nearby.

The passage opened into a small, hidden grotto bathed in a soft, ethereal glow. A tiny stream trickled through the grotto, its water sparkling with a gentle, shimmering light. The grotto's walls displayed exquisite crystals, their surfaces shimmering with a thousand rainbow hues. Jessica had never witnessed such a thing.

The grotto felt magical, imbued with ancient wonder. This hidden world was a secret sanctuary. While exploring the grotto, she uncovered a small, hidden cave behind a waterfall. Inside the cave, she found a collection of ancient-looking artifacts — crafted pottery shards, carved stones, and strange metallic objects whose purpose she couldn't decipher. These were not artifacts; they felt like relics of a long-lost civilization, carrying echoes of forgotten stories and whispers of ancient secrets.

Jessica spent the next few hours exploring the grotto and its hidden cave, sketching the artifacts and the breathtaking crystals that adorned it. She documented her findings, adding another chapter to her burgeoning encyclopedia of backyard wonders. As the sun set, casting long shadows through the grotto's entrance, she emerged from the hidden passage, her heart filled with excitement, wonder, and profound gratitude. The wind spirits' message had led her to an extraordinary discovery.

That evening, Jessica felt a renewed sense of wonder and appreciation for the boundless possibilities hidden within the ordinary. Her backyard wasn't a backyard anymore; it was a portal to a world of endless discovery, a canvas for her imagination to paint vivid and breathtaking landscapes. Uncovering a lost, well-unveiled kingdom; its magic is unexpected. The wind spirits, she realized, were not mischievous guardians; they were guides, leading her on a path of discovery, enriching her life with wonder and wonderment. She felt absolutely certain that many secrets and wonders awaited discovery in her vast, intriguing backyard. Her adventure, she knew, was far from over. The world presents itself as an unfolding narrative, each chapter a fresh adventure.

Chapter 15: Deciphering the Leaf's Riddle

Jessica turned the leaf in her hands, its ethereal glow captivating her. Unlike any alphabet she knew, the symbols pulsed with a faint, inner light, resonating with a strange familiarity. She felt a connection to them, a sense of understanding transcending the simple act of seeing. It was as if the leaf was whispering secrets, urging her to unravel its mysteries. Her fingertip traced the delicate lines, her mind racing with possibilities. Could these symbols be a code? A map? A language from a long-forgotten time?

The cryptic puzzle that tested both heart and mind, written beneath the symbols in elegant script, only intensified her curiosity. "Where the old well whispers secrets to the moon," it began, its words painting a vivid picture in her mind. She pictured the old well, its mossy stones, silent witnesses to passing time, behind the overgrown bushes. She had always considered it an old, neglected part of her yard, but now it felt different, alive with hidden potential.

The second line, "A hidden path awaits, beneath the silent noon," added another layer of intrigue. Silent noon. Was that midday? Perhaps it suggested a cryptic, suspenseful history. The poem's final two lines, "Seek the stone with three whispering chimes, a new adventure unfolds," persuaded her. This wasn't a game; it was an invitation, a challenging invitation to another layer of her extraordinary backyard.

The thought of three whispering chimes sent a shiver of excitement down her spine. Were they literal chimes hidden somewhere near the well? Or were they something else—a sound produced by the wind, whispering secrets, whistling through a peculiar formation of rocks, perhaps? The cryptic puzzle that tested both heart and mind felt almost alive, its words unfolding in her mind like a blossoming flower, revealing new layers of meaning with every rereading.

Jessica's excitement mounted. She grabbed her sketchbook, a magnifying glass—just in case the symbols needed closer examination—and a small trowel, perfect for clearing away any overgrown vegetation. They still effectively transitioned into a passage. She felt a surge of determination. This was an adventure, and she was ready to embrace it. Reaching the well proved difficult. A dense tangle of weeds, vines, and brambles overgrew the path.

Thorns snagged at her clothes, and insects buzzed around her head, but she pressed on, her determination fueled by the promise of discovery. She imagined herself as one of the explorers in the documentary she'd watched, clearing a path through the untamed wilderness, her spirit undaunted by the obstacles she encountered. Each step forward felt like a victory, a testament to her courage and resolve.

Archaeologists uncovered the ancient well. Moss and ivy covered the aged and weathered stonework. The well itself was dark and still, its water reflecting the sky like a mysterious mirror. It was a silent sentinel, a testament to time, its stoic presence radiating an aura of age-old secrets.

Jessica reread the cryptic puzzle that tested both heart and mind, her eyes scanning the well's mossy surface. She circled the well, running her fingers over the rough texture of the stones, searching for any irregularities, any hint of a hidden passage. She peered into the dark depths of the water, but saw nothing beyond its murky surface. The cryptic puzzle spoke of a hidden path; she was determined to find it. She pondered, "Where the old well whispers secrets to the moon," considering the moonlight's potential in revealing the passage.

Her gaze fell upon a section of the wells back, half-concealed by a sprawling bramble bush. The sprawling bramble bush almost hid the stonework's narrow cleft, wide enough for her hand. The small opening may have seemed insignificant, but it carried a profound significance, echoing the cryptic words of the challenging puzzle that tested both the heart and mind. She knew this was it. With renewed vigor, she set about clearing the brambles away.

Thorns scratched at her arms, and her fingers grew sore, but she persisted, her determination unwavering. She pulled away the thick, intertwining branches, revealing the small passage. It was a narrow opening, large enough to squeeze through, but that didn't deter her. It was the path, the secret route revealed by the wind, whispering secret spirits' cryptic puzzle that tested both heart and mind.

As she peered into the opening, her heart pounded in her chest. The passage was enigmatic, hinting at secrets beyond comprehension. But a sense of excitement propelled her forward, a potent mixture of fear and exhilaration. She sought a new adventure, a chance to explore the magic of her backyard further.

She took a deep breath, braced herself, and slipped through the narrow opening. The passage was claustrophobic, the air cool and damp against her skin. The sounds of the world outside faded away, replaced by a gentle hush, a profound silence that spoke volumes. She continued, her hands brushing against rough, uneven stone, her progress slow but deliberate. As she journeyed on, the surrounding magic seemed to quicken.

Opening into a small, hidden grotto, the passage caused her to gasp in surprise as her eyes adjusted to the dim light. The grotto was breathtaking. Tiny lights seemed to be embedded within its depths, as a small stream trickled through the center, its water sparkling with a faint, ethereal glow. The grotto's walls shimmered with exquisite crystals, their surfaces refracting the light into a kaleidoscope of colors. Each crystal seemed to hold its unique spectrum, a miniature universe of light and color. It was a sight more magnificent than she could have ever imagined. This was beyond the wonders she had found beneath her porch. This was a hidden sanctuary, a secret treasure nestled deep within the heart of her backyard.

And then, she heard the sound—a gentle tinkling, a soft chime audible yet clear. She looked around, her heart pounding with excitement. Hidden behind a waterfall's curtain, she spotted three small stones nestled within the rock's niche. As she reached out and touched them, each stone emitted a delicate, almost ethereal chime, confirming the cryptic puzzle that tested both heart and mind's last clue. She uncovered the three whispering chimes.

The discovery deepened her wonder. Time-smoothed stones via water. Their surfaces reflected light, and the subtle hues within the rocks seemed to change with the movement of the water. They were unlike any stones she had ever seen before. These weren't rocks; they were magical artifacts protecting this secret place.

Beyond the waterfall, another wonder awaited. A small cave opened behind the cascading water, its entrance shrouded in mist. Her curiosity propelled her forward, and she stepped into the lit cave, her heart filled with anticipation.

Inside, she found a treasure trove of artifacts—crafted pottery shards, carved stones, and strange metallic objects whose purpose remained a mystery. Intricate patterns adorned the pottery pieces, and the rocks displayed carvings of such complexity that they suggested a skill level surpassing anything she had ever seen. The metallic objects were sleek and smooth, almost otherworldly, and some emitted faint vibrations, like a low hum.

These were not ordinary artifacts; they felt ancient and powerful, imbued with a history stretching back countless years.

She spent the rest of the afternoon exploring the grotto and the hidden cave, sketching the artifacts and the crystals, marveling at their beauty and complexity. She documented everything, adding another layer to her growing encyclopedia of backyard wonders. As the sun set, casting long shadows across the grotto's entrance, Jessica emerged, feeling invigorated, inspired, and grateful. Her amazing adventure began with a wind spirit puzzle. Her backyard was more than a backyard; it was a limitless realm of possibilities, a place where imagination knew no bounds. She was ready to begin an excellent new chapter, and the world awaited her story.

Chapter 16: Boarding the Swing Set Ship

The three whispering chimes hummed a silent melody in Jessica's ears, a lingering echo of the magical grotto. She emerged from the hidden passage, blinking in the sudden brightness of the afternoon sun. That former well reflects her journey's transformation. But her exploration wasn't over. Another mystery emerged—the transformation of her swing set into a pirate ship, an idea that had been brewing in her mind since she uncovered the wind, whispering secret spirits' cryptic puzzle that tested both heart and mind.

A simple structure made of wood and chains transformed before her eyes. Shimmering and morphing, the wooden frame of the swing set became the sturdy hull of a magnificent galleon. The rusty chains changed into thick hemp ropes, replacing the metallic clang with the rhythmic creak of aged wood. The worn-out seats were gone, replaced by strong decks ready to support the weight of her crew and treasure. Sturdy masts and billowing sails appeared, along with a proud Jolly Roger fluttering from the highest point of the ship.

Her trusty companion, Whiskers, her hamster, scampered from her pocket, his tiny nose twitching. He was her first mate, her loyal companion, on this fantastical voyage. Jessica scooped him up, cradling him in her hands. "Ahoy, matey!" she whispered, her voice brimming with excitement. Whiskers, understanding her enthusiasm, twitched his whiskers and let out a tiny squeak that Jessica interpreted as a hearty, "Aye, Captain!"

She started the transformation, using her imagination as a key tool. She gathered fallen leaves, twigs, and flowers, fashioning them into makeshift sails and decorations. The leaves, vibrant with autumnal hues, formed a patchwork sail, each one a unique tile in a breathtaking mural. She used colored ribbons and scraps of fabric, salvaged from old projects, to add a touch of flair to her ship's rigging. The rope swing, used for languid swaying, became the ship's sturdy mainmast. Her pet rock, a smooth, gray stone she'd carried around since she was little, became the ship's figurehead–Captain Rock, a fearless guardian of the high seas. She affixed him to the front of the swing set, his stoic face seeming to gaze towards the horizon of her imagined ocean.

The backyard transformed. The lush green lawn transformed into a boundless ocean, its undulating surface shimmering in the midday sun. Tall grasses swayed, imitating the gentle rocking of waves against the ship's hull. The flowerbeds, teeming with vibrant blooms, became exotic islands, their colorful petals forming a unique archipelago in her imaginary sea. Even the towering oak tree at the edge of the yard, a mere backdrop, now loomed as a formidable cliff, its ancient branches forming a rugged coastline.

Jessica, her imagination running wild, fashioned a small wooden box into a treasure chest, filled with her most prized possessions: smooth, colorful pebbles she had collected from the creek behind her house, buttons, and a few colorful bottle caps. These were her pirate treasures, the spoils of many imagined adventures.

With her pirate ship ready, Jessica, her heart pounding with excitement, climbed aboard. Whiskers, nestled in a miniature hammock she'd crafted from a scrap of cloth, watched intently, almost as if understanding every move from his vantage point. "All hands on deck!" she declared, her voice echoing in the quiet afternoon.

She hoisted her makeshift sails; the wind whispering secrets (a gentle breeze rustling through the trees) catching them with surprising efficiency. The swing set creaked and swayed, mimicking the motion of a ship in the waves. She gripped the ropes, feeling the thrill of the simulated voyage. The imaginary ocean stretched before her, inviting her to explore its depths.

Navigating the 'grassy seas' proved to be an interesting trial with hidden stakes. Jessica had to maneuver her ship, avoiding the 'rocky reefs' formed by clumps of sturdy grass. She used a long stick as a makeshift rudder, guiding her ship with skillful precision. She even devised a signaling system using colored flags, cut from fabric scraps, to signal imaginary ships she encountered during her journey.

A stubborn patch of dandelions posed a significant hazard, threatening to capsize her ship. Jessica, with remarkable resourcefulness, dug around the offending plants with her trowel, creating a makeshift channel through which she could sail her vessel.

She spotted a flock of butterflies flitting among the flowers on one of her imaginary islands. These weren't ordinary butterflies; they shimmered with iridescent colors, their wings adorned with patterns that resembled miniature maps. Jessica decided they were her scouts, reporting back on the condition of the seas. She followed their flight pattern, guided by their purposeful movements, and uncovered a hidden grove of wild raspberries — a sweet reward for her daring voyage.

As she sailed along, she encountered friendly creatures along the way–a family of ants marching in a single file across a leaf, their tiny legs moving with extraordinary determination; a ladybug perched on a blade of grass, its shell gleaming; and a friendly spider spinning a glistening web between two flower stalks. Each encounter added an extra dimension to her adventure, turning every moment into a thrilling experience.

As the sun dipped below the horizon, casting long shadows across her backyard ocean, Jessica brought her ship into port. Her 'grassy seas' had been a vast, exciting expanse, filled with unique challenges and rewarding discoveries. Exhaustion and exhilaration filled her, her heart brimming with the joy of her creative journey.

She secured her ship (the swing set) for the night, promising herself many more voyages across her imaginary oceans. Drowsy from his adventure, Whiskers snuggled into his hammock, a contented sigh escaping his tiny chest. Jessica gathered her treasures, placing them back in her makeshift treasure chest. The pebbles, buttons, and bottle caps seemed to gleam with a newfound brilliance, charged with the magic of her afternoon adventure.

She smiled, her eyes sparkling with the magic she had created. Once a simple space, her backyard was now a realm of endless possibilities, a testament to the power of imagination. The wind spirits' cryptic puzzle that tested both heart and mind led her to a hidden grotto, unlocking a new level of creativity and transforming her ordinary swing set into an extraordinary adventure vessel. The world, she knew, was brimming with untold stories, and she, the intrepid explorer of her backyard, was ready to uncover them all. She looked forward to tomorrow, another day filled with exciting adventures in her fantastic world.

Chapter 17: Aboard the Pirate Ship, The Seagulls' Song

As the sun fell, long shadows stretched across the temporary ocean. As she sat on the deck of her pirate ship, admiring the sunset that painted the sky in hues of orange and purple, she noticed something unusual. Three seagulls, their feathers gleaming like polished silver, perched on the railing of her vessel, the sturdy frame of the swing set. They weren't ordinary seagulls; these birds seemed to possess an almost human intelligence, their bright eyes shining with mischief.

One seagull, larger than the others, let out a series of sharp, high-pitched cries. It wasn't squawking; it was a song, a melodic sequence of calls and whistles that resonated with Jessica, weaving a strange, captivating tune. The other two seagulls chimed in, their voices harmonizing with the leader, creating a complex and enchanting melody. As the song unfolded, Jessica recognized that the melody had a hidden meaning. She listened, trying to decipher the coded message carried on the sea breeze. It was like a cryptic puzzle that tested both heart and mind, a playful trial with hidden stakes whispered by the wind, whispering secrets. The song spoke of a hidden treasure, a secret prize awaiting discovery on a distant island.

The lyrics, translated in Jessica's mind, seemed to describe a journey to the sandbox, now transformed in her imagination into a tropical island teeming with exotic flora and fauna. It spoke of a path hidden beneath a blanket of colorful flowers, leading to a cave concealed within the island's sandy shores.

"A treasure awaits where sunbeams play, hidden beneath the blooms and where sandpipers stray." Jessica interpreted this as a rhyme inspired by the song of a seagull. She realized that the "sunbeams" referred to the patch of sunlight illuminating her sandbox, showing the location of the hidden path. She understood the clue.

Whiskers, her ever-present first mate, stirred in his hammock. He peered at the seagulls with his tiny black eyes, seeming to share Jessica's excitement. He twitched his whiskers, as if agreeing with her song interpretation. "Aye, Captain!" she whispered to her furry companion, confirming her belief that she had decoded the seagull's message.

Jessica lowered her makeshift sails. The wind sighed as the fall leaves quivered and settled around her. She climbed down from the swing set, her heart pounding with anticipation. The seagulls remained perched on the ship, their watchful gaze following her every move. They seemed to be her guides, her avian companions on this new leg of her adventure.

She approached the sandbox, her footsteps placed among the blooming marigolds and zinnias, the vibrant colors of the flowerbed seeming to pulsate with an otherworldly glow. The sandbox was no longer a box filled with sand; it was now a lush tropical island, a miniature paradise complete with palm trees (her father's gardening tools positioned), and sandy beaches.

The seagulls' song pointed to a hidden path within the lush flowerbed. Following the clues, Jessica noticed a subtle shift in the flower arrangement—a less dense area, almost like a secret pathway concealed within the dense blooms. She parted the flowers, revealing a narrow passage leading towards the sandy shores of her island.

The path was visible, but Jessica's keen eyes picked up the trail. It was a labyrinth of tunnels and trails winding through the flowerbed. Each turn brought new challenges—weaving between swaying petals, stepping over vibrant blossoms, and avoiding prickly stems.

The flowers seemed to shimmer with a faint, ethereal light, as if acknowledging her passage. She felt a sense of wonder, as if the plants were guiding her, their fragrant petals offering a delicate perfume that filled the air with a mystical scent. As she made her way through the maze of flowers, Jessica noticed tiny, sparkling crystals embedded in the petals of some blooms. They were like miniature jewels, shimmering in the fading light of the afternoon sun, catching the last rays of sunlight before dusk. She collected a few, marveling at their delicate beauty. They were unlike anything she had ever seen.

The path led her to the edge of the sandbox, where she uncovered a small cave hidden within the sandy embankment. The cave opening, concealed by a trailing vine, was large enough for her to squeeze through. Having followed her progress from their vantage point on the ship, the seagulls swooped down and perched near the cave entrance, as if approving of her progress.

Taking a deep breath, Jessica crawled into the cave. It was darker inside, but she had brought a small flashlight from her room, anticipating the possibility of a darker path. The cave walls were smooth and calm, the sand soft beneath her fingertips. Inside, stillness reigned, unlike the lively backyard.

As her eyes adjusted to the dimness, she saw a small, wooden chest nestled in a recess within the cave wall. Intricate carvings depicting sailing ships and mythical creatures decorated the chest. It was far more ornate than the treasure chest she had crafted for her pirate ship. The sight filled Jessica with excitement and a sense of accomplishment. She had found the treasure.

She opened the chest, her heart pounding with anticipation. Inside, nestled on a bed of soft velvet, she found a collection of glittering gems, smooth colorful stones, and tiny seashells, each unique and sparkling. Magical trinkets overflowed, surpassing her wildest dreams.

She found a small, carved wooden whistle among the jewels, similar to the one she'd uncovered in the grotto. This one, however, seemed to hum with a faint, ethereal energy. She blew into the whistle, and a soft, melodic tune unlike any she had heard before filled the air. It was a lullaby, gentle and the perfect end to her exciting pirate adventure.

Jessica closed the chest, her heart filled with gratitude and joy. She had solved the cryptic puzzle and uncovered a treasure far exceeding her wildest dreams. As she left the cave, the seagulls greeted her with another series of melodious calls, a triumphant song celebrating her successful quest. She knew this wasn't the end of her adventures.

Her magical backyard world held many more treasures and mysteries to uncover. The setting sun painted the sky in fiery hues as she returned to her pirate ship, eager for another journey in her boundless, imaginative realm. The whispered secrets of the sea, the songs of the wind, whispering secrets, and the treasures of her enchanted backyard awaited her. Her exploration was far from over; more dreams and adventures beckoned.

Chapter 18: The Sandbox Island and Its Treasure

The path, wider than her outstretched hands, wound through a riot of color. Marigolds, their faces turned toward the sun, seemed to wink at her as she passed. In shades of fiery orange and deep crimson, zinnias swayed in the late afternoon breeze, their petals brushing against her cheeks like whispered secrets. The air hummed with the buzz of bees, drunk on the nectar of the blossoms, and the sweet scent of honeysuckle hung heavy in the air. It wasn't a flower bed anymore; it was a fragrant, vibrant jungle, a miniature Eden crafted by her imagination.

Each step was a careful negotiation, a delicate dance between her eagerness and the intricacies of her floral pathway. Protecting the blossoms required her to avoid unseen thorns. Sometimes, she had to crawl, squeezing between dense clusters of blooms. Other times, she had to lift a curtain of petals to reveal the next section of her path, like a secret hidden behind a velvety, fragrant veil.

It felt like the flowers were guiding her, their petals parting to reveal the way forward. The air seemed charged with a magical energy, a playful, encouraging hum that whispered of adventure and discovery. She noticed tiny, glittering dewdrops clinging to the petals, catching the remaining rays of the setting sun, and scattering them like miniature rainbows. These weren't ordinary dewdrops; they shimmered with an otherworldly glow, like tiny, captured stars.

As she ventured deeper, she uncovered small, smooth stones embedded within the soil at the base of the plants. Each stone was a different color—some were the deep, earthy brown of the soil itself, others a vibrant, sun-kissed yellow, and still others shimmered with a pearly, opalescent glow. They felt warm to the touch, like sunbaked treasures. Jessica pocketed a few of these stones, adding them to her growing collection of magical artifacts.

She would encounter a massive bloom, almost like a giant velvety goblet, filled to the brim with dew. She'd peer inside, expecting to find some hidden treasure, some magical secret within its depths. The shimmering dewdrops captivated her, but the excitement of seeking was just as satisfying as the joy of discovering.

The path led her to the edge of the sandbox; the sand shimmering golden in the late afternoon light. It wasn't sand anymore; it was a fine, white beach, its surface undisturbed, except for the occasional, tiny footprint of some unseen creature. She could almost feel the warmth of the sun on her skin, feel the fine grains of sand between her toes, though, of course, the reality was the cool touch of the wood framing the sandbox.

The seagulls, her aerial companions, swooped down and landed on the edge of the sandbox, their silvery feathers gleaming like polished coins in the fading light. They seemed to approve of her progress, their bright eyes following her every move. Their presence provided a comforting reassurance, a sense that she was indeed on the right path, that her adventure was unfolding as it should.

She noticed a slight indentation in the sand, almost hidden beneath a trailing vine, imperceptible against the backdrop of the sun-drenched sand. She parted the vine, revealing a small opening, a tiny mouth leading into the earth. It was a small and dark cave, yet promising and beckoning her to explore its secrets.

Taking a deep breath, Jessica crawled into the cave. The refreshing coolness of the air was a welcome change from the oppressive heat. The walls were smooth, the sand soft beneath her hands. She brought her small flashlight to bear, its beam cutting through the darkness to reveal the cave's interior. The cave was spacious, larger than she thought. Some of the fascinating rock formations mimicked strange creatures, while swirling clouds adorned the walls. She wondered how the simple shifting and settling of sand could have produced such intricate forms.

She saw a small wooden chest deep within the cave, nestled in a small alcove. Intricate carvings adorned the chest's surface, depicting fantastical creatures and sailing ships with tiny masts reaching towards an imagined sky. The artifact appeared ancient, unearthed after eons. That chest surpassed all others she'd encountered; its beauty exceeded even the play chests in toy stores.

With trembling hands, Jessica opened the chest. Instead of gold coins or jewels, she found something even more precious: a collection of smooth, colorful seashells. Ocean waves shaped each shell into a unique, miniature work of art. There were spiral shells, their curves swirling inwards like miniature galaxies, and ribbed shells, their surfaces textured with delicate lines. There were tiny, pearly shells, their surfaces shimmering with a rainbow of colors. Then she spotted a small, smooth, gray stone hidden inside the chest. It wasn't like the other stones she had found along the flower path. This stone felt different, warm to the touch, almost alive. As she held it, she felt a strange tingling sensation in her hand, a sense of connection, of sharing warmly, weaving their stories into her world of energy.

She knew this stone was special, holding some unique power and hidden magic. It felt like a piece of her imagination, solidified, given form. She felt a deep connection to this ordinary stone.

As she closed the chest and emerged from the cave, the seagulls cried out overhead. The setting sun cast long shadows across the sandbox, transforming it into a magical landscape bathed in golden light. Jessica's treasure surpassed a mere seashell collection. The whispers of the wind, whispering secrets, the songs of the birds, and the secrets of her enchanted backyard would continue to guide, inspire, and invite her on countless more expeditions into the limitless realm of her imagination. She clutched the gray stone in her hand, a tangible reminder of her magical journey and a promise of many more adventures to come.

Chapter 19: The Map to the Wishing Well

The gray stone felt warm against her palm, pulsing with a gentle warmth that spread through her hand and up her arm. It wasn't a stone, but a key — a magical conduit to another layer of her backyard's enchanted reality. As she held it, the seashells in the chest seemed to shimmer, their colors intensifying, their surfaces reflecting the last rays of the setting sun like tiny mirrors catching the celestial fire. A thrill sparked beneath her skin, a thrilling anticipation that sent a shiver of delight down her spine.

She re-closed the ornate chest, its carvings now seeming to shift and writhe before her eyes, as if the tiny ships etched onto its surface were preparing to set sail. She placed it back in the alcove, feeling a strange sense of responsibility, a guardianship over this hidden treasure. The cave seemed to sigh around her, a quiet exhalation of ancient secrets.

Back out in the sandbox-turned-beach, the seagulls had taken flight, their calls echoing across her miniature world. As the sun dipped below the horizon, a refreshing coolness settled over the land. As she left the cave, brushing aside the trailing vine that concealed its entrance, her hand brushed against something else — a small, rolled parchment tucked beneath the vine. Time and exposure to the elements had aged and made it brittle, fraying, and softening its edges. She unfurled it, revealing a map drawn with delicate lines that looked like charcoal or perhaps sepia ink.

The map was unlike any she had ever seen. It wasn't a detailed geographical chart but a whimsical, almost dreamlike representation of her backyard. The map depicted the oak tree, her mountain, as a towering peak, its branches reaching towards a sky filled with swirling stars. She rendered her swing set; her pirate ship, in exquisite detail, drawing its ropes and sails with precision. She depicted the flowerbeds, her jungle, as a lush, vibrant green expanse, punctuated by bursts of color that reflected the fresh flowers within.

But what captivated her attention was a winding path, depicted in shimmering silver ink, leading away from her sandbox beach and towards a small, circular symbol nestled within a grove of whispering willows at the far end of her yard. The symbol itself was enigmatic: a simple circle surrounding a smaller, inner circle, adorned with delicate, looping lines that suggested water flowing. Below the emblem, matching the map's elegant script, read: "Wishing Well."

A gasp escaped her lips. A wishing well! She had heard stories about wishing wells, places where dreams come true, where the whispers of hopes and desires ascended to the heavens. Of course, she had never believed in them. But now, holding this map, standing in her transformed backyard, the possibility felt real. The map wasn't a guide; it was an invitation, a trial with hidden stakes, a beckoning towards the unknown. Her heart beat faster, a drum of excitement thrumming against her ribs. This was more than an adventure; it was a quest, a journey towards something magical.

She tucked the map into her pocket and turned towards the willows. Her pirate ship loomed before her, its wooden planks now seeming to glow with a warm, inviting light. She climbed aboard, her legs swinging as she settled onto the swing, feeling the familiar rhythm of her journey. Overhead, her faithful companions, the seagulls, circled, their cries sounding like joyous encouragement.

The trip to the wishing well proved quite adventurous. The map depicted a path that wasn't easy. It led her through a maze of tall grasses that tickled her legs and whispered secrets in the evening breeze. She had to navigate around a patch of thorny blackberry bushes, their wicked spines reaching out like grasping claws. She avoided the grumpy old gnome who lived beneath the hydrangea bush, his tiny beard bristling. He grumbled something about noisy children and disturbed naps, but she smiled and offered him a juicy raspberry, which seemed to pacify him.

Once past the grumpy gnome, she uncovered a hidden stream, more than a trickle, but still a stream, meandering its way through the grass. The water was crystal clear, reflecting the fading sunlight like a ribbon of liquid light. She followed its course, stepping across smooth, moss-covered stones, each cool and slick beneath her bare feet.

The map guided her through a dense thicket of rosebushes, their blossoms rioting in pink and red. Their fragrance filled the air, a heady perfume that made her feel as though she were floating on a cloud of petals. She had to use her imagination to see the path, following the faded silver strokes on the map as if they were alive and guiding her to her destination.

The air grew cooler as she approached the grove of whispering willows, their branches reaching out like skeletal arms, their leaves rustling with a soft, almost musical whisper. The map showed the Wishing Well at the center of this grove. A hush fell upon the air as she stepped beneath the weeping willows, a profound silence that she could almost hear her heartbeat. Sunlight dappled the ground, swinging shadows.

And then she saw it.

The roots of the oldest willow nestled around a well, hidden by drooping branches. It wasn't a simple well, like the ones she had seen in pictures or movies. This was a magical well, its stone rim encrusted with glistening crystals, the water within swirling with an ethereal luminescence. The water was not water; it shimmered with an inner light, like a miniature galaxy trapped within a stone basin.

The air hummed with a low, resonant thrum, a vibration that seemed to resonate deep within her bones. She felt a sense of awe, wonder, and a profound connection to this magical place. This wasn't a well, a portal, a gateway to dreams. The map had led her to this enchanted spot where, she believed, the impossible might become possible. The gray stone, warm in her pocket, pulsed with a stronger beat, as if confirming magic all around her. She knew, with a certainty beyond logic or reason, that her adventure was far from over. The wishing well awaited, a silent promise of untold possibilities.

Chapter 20: The Journey to the Wishing Well

Although marked on the ancient map, the path was no simple stroll. The map revealed the location of the Wishing Well and the obstacles Jessica would encounter on her journey. This wasn't a mere walk in the park; this was a test, a trial of sorts, designed to prove her worthiness, her readiness to make a wish.

First came the whispering grasses, tall and swaying, their blades tickling her legs like mischievous fingers. Their whispers, a sibilant chorus, resembled laughter. Jessica giggled, their playful antics contrasting with the serious task. She imagined tiny grass sprites, laughing and dancing among the stalks, their laughter echoing in the evening air.

She parted the grasses, creating a path through their swaying ranks, a tiny explorer forging through a verdant jungle. Next, the thorny blackberry bushes presented a more formidable trial with hidden stakes. Ripe, dark berries laden their tangled, interwoven branches, forming an impenetrable barrier. The map showed a narrow passage, a hidden gap between two dense clusters of land.

With cautious fingers, she pushed aside the thorny, tender grinds, her breath held, skin prickling with fear and excitement. She found a narrow passage; She emerged on the other side, triumphant, with a few minor scratches, her only reward for her bravery.

The grumpy gnome, depicted on the map as a tiny, scowling figure beneath the hydrangea bush, proved to be as cantankerous as he appeared. This gnome, unusually large, sported a beard like a tangled bird's nest; his eyes narrowed to slits at her approach. He grumbled something about noisy children disturbing his afternoon nap, his voice a low, guttural rumble. Jessica, remembering the kindness of her neighbors, employed diplomacy. She offered him one of the plump, juicy raspberries she had picked from the blackberry bushes, a peace offering. The gnome accepted the offering, his scowl softening as he popped the berry into his mouth. He mumbled something that sounded like a reluctant thank you, then returned to his nap, his grumbling reduced to a low, sleepy hum.

Beyond the gnome's domain, she encountered a hidden stream, wider than her hand, but sparkling with crystalline clarity. The map showed the stream's path, winding its way through the grass, and Jessica followed its silvery course, careful not to disturb the delicate ecosystem that thrived along its banks. She spotted tiny, iridescent dragonflies flitting over the water's surface and miniature frogs, the size of her thumb, leaping from one smooth, moss-covered stone to another. She hopped from stone to stone, careful to avoid disturbing the delicate balance of this miniature world. Washing away the weariness of her journey, the refreshing water against her feet seemed to invigorate her. The setting sun cast long shadows that stretched and danced along the banks, transforming the humble stream into a magical, shimmering ribbon of light.

Fragrant and colorful, the rose bushes presented yet another trial with hidden stakes. Heavy with blooms, their branches formed a dense, almost impenetrable thicket. The map again provided the key, showing a faint trail winding through the fragrant labyrinth. Jessica navigated the maze, careful not to snag her clothes on the thorns, her senses overwhelmed by the intoxicating perfume of the roses. She inhaled, the sweet scent filling her lungs, making her feel as though she were drifting on a cloud of petals. Navigating the thorny path became easier thanks to the roses' beauty, colors, and fragrance. The map guided her through this fragrant maze, a testament to its magical nature.

She reached the grove of whispering willows, their branches draped towards the ground like weeping mourners. Cooler air settled in, sunlight filtering through the dense foliage to create a dappled pattern on the ground. The rustling of the leaves, a constant whisper, created an atmosphere of quiet mystery. The map showed the Wishing Well nestled at the heart of the grove, and Jessica, her heart pounding with anticipation, pushed aside the lowest-hanging branches.

And there it was.

The Wishing Well was even more beautiful than she could have imagined. Swirling patterns carved its stone rim, which was encrusted with shimmering crystals sparkling like captured starlight. Far from still, the water within swirled, its surface shimmering with an ethereal luminescence. Pulsating with a soft, inner light, the water seemed to glow like a miniature galaxy in a stone basin.

The air hummed with a low, resonant thrum, a vibration deep within her chest, a palpable sense of magic filling the air.

Pulses of warmth from the gray stone in her pocket echoed the surrounding magic. This wasn't a wishing well; it was a portal, a gateway to the realm of dreams, a testament to the power of her imagination. The map led her to wonder and possibility, not a location. She knew, with absolute certainty, that her adventure was far from over; the wishing well awaited, a silent promise of the magical possibilities ahead.

Chapter 21: Jessica Shares Her Adventures with Mom

The whispering willows seemed to bid farewell as Jessica emerged from the grove. The gray stone warm against her palm was a tangible reminder of her incredible journey. She felt lighter than air, her heart thrumming with exhilaration and contentment. The sun, now sinking below the horizon, painted the sky in vibrant hues of orange and purple, casting long shadows that stretched and danced across her backyard. It wasn't her backyard anymore; it was a kingdom, a world she had explored and conquered.

A familiar warmth greeted her as she approached the back door—the comforting aroma of her mother's cooking, a blend of garlic, oregano, and something sweet. She burst through the door, her cheeks flushed with excitement, her eyes shining with the residual magic of her adventure.

"Mom! Mom!" she exclaimed, echoing through the kitchen.

Her mother, humming as she stirred a pot on the stove, turned, her face breaking into a warm smile. "Jessica, darling! You're back! How was your exploration?"

Jessica launched into a detailed account of her journey. Her description included the whispering grasses, their playful antics, and the secrets they seemed to share. She recounted her daring escape from the thorny blackberry bushes, the encounter with the grumpy gnome (and his surprising fondness for raspberries), and the delicate beauty of the hidden stream, with its iridescent dragonflies and miniature frogs.

Speaking of the rose bushes, she described a fragrant and colorful maze that challenged her navigation skills. Her words painted vivid pictures of the intoxicating perfume that filled the air. Her voice rose and fell with the rhythm of her story, her hands gesturing as she recreated the scene, and her eyes sparkling with the memory of the adventure.

"I found the Wishing Well!" she whispered.

Her mother leaned forward; her eyes were wide with interest. "The Wishing Well? Tell me everything!"

Jessica described the well, her voice filled with awe. She painted a picture of the carved stone rim, the shimmering crystals that sparkled like captured starlight, and the swirling, luminous water within. She talked about the magic that permeated the air, the resonant thrum that vibrated through her chest, and her profound connection to the place.

"It was... magical, Mom," she said, her voice catching in her throat. "Like something out of a fairy tale."

Her mother listened, her eyes reflecting the wonder in her daughter's voice. She didn't interrupt; she didn't dismiss it as a childish fantasy. Instead, she encouraged her, asking questions, drawing her out, helping her to weave the story into a rich tapestry of imagination and adventure.

"And what did you wish for?" her mother asked, when Jessica paused for breath.

Jessica hesitated for a moment. She hadn't made a wish yet. The well's enchantment held her captive; she couldn't wish it away. The act felt like it might diminish the wonder of it.

"I... I haven't wished yet," she admitted, a little. "It felt too special, too magical. I wanted to savor the moment, you know? I felt like it was too precious to ruin with a wish."

Her mother smiled. "That's alright, darling. Some things are more precious than a wish. It sounds like you had an incredible adventure, a true journey of the heart and imagination."

Jessica beamed. She felt a surge of warmth and validation, a deep sense of being understood and cherished. Her mother didn't listen; she saw and heard her, her imagination, and her adventure. She wasn't a listener but a participant in the wonder. They sat at the kitchen table, the aroma of the simmering stew filling the air, and Jessica continued her story, adding details, embellishments, and discoveries she had only realized. She told her mother about the gray stone, how it had pulsed with warmth during the most magical moments of her journey, a constant reminder of the magic she had encountered.

She described the tiny details—the way the sunlight dappled through the leaves, the patterns of moss on the stones by the stream, the iridescent sheen of the dragonflies' wings, and the grumpy gnome's kind acceptance of the raspberry. Each detail recounted, painted a vivid picture of her extraordinary adventure in the ordinary backyard. Her mother listened, interjecting with questions that deepened the story, adding layers of detail and emotion. It wasn't a retelling of events; it was a collaborative effort.

As the story unfolded, Jessica's mother noticed something peculiar about the gray stone. It seemed to glow in the kitchen light, emitting a soft, ethereal radiance. She picked it up, turning it over in her hands. It felt warm to the touch, almost pulsating with a gentle energy.

"This stone... It's amazing," she murmured, her voice filled with wonder. "It seems to have its magic."

Jessica nodded. "I knew it! I told you it was magical!"

That evening, conversation flowed; topics ranged from imaginative power and natural beauty to the value of believing in the extraordinary, not Jessica's adventures. The kitchen, filled with the aroma of the stew and the warmth of their conversation, became a haven of sharing warmly, weaving their stories into her world of wonder, a space where imagination could flourish and dreams could take flight. Their extraordinary evening left the gray stone resting on the kitchen table, a silent testament to the magic found in the most unexpected places and the power of sharing warmly, weaving their stories into her world experience to amplify that magic tenfold.

The next day, Jessica showed her grandmother her drawings of the fantastical creatures and places she'd encountered, and her grandmother, wise and knowing, listened with the same attentive fascination as her mother had. Her grandmother, a storyteller, added her magical tales to Jessica's.

The adventures continued, with her grandmother sharing her childhood memories of exploring her own "magical" backyard—a forgotten orchard behind her house she had transformed into her enchanted realm of secret paths, hidden nooks, and chattering birds. She befriended the local wildlife, finding solace in nature, mirroring Jessica's garden sanctuary. It was like the magic had passed from generation to generation, a precious heirloom of imagination and wonder.

They had magical tales about hidden caves, whispering rivers, mystical creatures, and ancient trees. Their unique perspectives added depth and richness, creating a tapestry of global wonder. Jessica learned that geography or language did not limit magic, wonder, and the spirit of adventure; they were universal elements of the human experience, woven into the fabric of childhood and imagination. Each story fueled her creativity and expanded her world, enriching her adventures and making them all the more captivating. The gray stone, now a family heirloom, remained a constant reminder of their collective journeys into the realms of fantasy. The backyard, now a place of vibrant wonder, held countless more adventures waiting to be discovered.

Chapter 22: Grandma's Storytelling and Wisdom

The next day dawned bright and sunny, promising another day of adventure. But this time, Jessica felt a different kind of excitement bubbling inside her. There was another person she longed to tell–her grandmother, Nana Rose. Nana Rose wasn't any grandmother; she was a weaver of tales, a keeper of secrets, a woman whose stories could transport you to lands beyond imagination. Jessica knew that Nana Rose would understand. She wouldn't just listen; she'd see the magic, too.

With her sketchbook filled with drawings of the grumpy gnome, the whispering willows, and the shimmering Wishing Well, Jessica skipped to her grandmother's house. A few blocks away sits a charming little cottage. The scent of baked bread wafted from the open window, a welcoming aroma that promised warmth and comfort.

Nana Rose greeted Jessica with a warm hug, her eyes twinkling with a familiar light of mischievous wisdom. "My adventurous granddaughter!" she exclaimed, her voice a comforting melody. "I've been waiting to hear all about your amazing discoveries!"

Jessica, perched on Nana Rose's comfortable armchair, unfolded her sketchbook, her fingers tracing the lines of her drawings. Her voice animated, eyes sparkling with remnants of her magical experience, she recounted her journey. She described the talking butterflies, their delicate wings shimmering like stained glass, the miniature frogs singing their tiny songs, and the grumpy gnome, whose initial grumpiness melted away upon being offered a juicy raspberry.

A maze of fragrant rose bushes; She spoke of the hidden stream, its waters shimmering with an ethereal glow, and the giant oak tree's branches reaching towards the heavens like ancient arms. She recounted her challenges, the cryptic puzzle that tested both heart and minds she had solved, and the sense of accomplishment that filled her heart. As Jessica spoke, Nana Rose listened, her gaze never leaving Jessica's face. She nodded, her eyes mirroring the wonder in Jessica's voice. When Jessica caught her breath, Nana Rose smiled, a knowing smile that suggested she understood the magic Jessica had experienced.

"My dear," Nana Rose said, her voice soothing, "your backyard sounds enchanted. It reminds me of my childhood adventures."

Jessica's eyes widened. "You had adventures, Nana?"

Nana Rose chuckled, a warm, comforted sound. "Oh, yes, my dear. Many adventures. I grew up in a small town surrounded by orchards and forests. Behind our house was an old orchard, overgrown and forgotten. To me, it was a magical kingdom." Nana Rose leaned forward, her eyes sparkling with memories. She told her stories, tales of hidden paths winding through overgrown apple trees, their branches laden with juicy, sun-ripened fruit. She spoke of secret nooks where she would build tiny homes for imaginary creatures, creating fantastical worlds amidst the tangled branches and rustling leaves.

She encountered playful squirrels with bushy tails twitching as they scampered, and wise old owls watching over her. She described the feeling of sunlight filtering through the leaves, dappling the ground in shifting patterns of light and shadow. She spoke of building rafts from fallen branches and sailing them down a meandering stream that flowed through the orchard, her laughter echoing through the trees.

Nana Rose filled her stories with a similar sense of wonder and magic that Jessica had experienced in her backyard. She described how the sunlight played amongst the trees, creating an ethereal glow that transformed the ordinary into the extraordinary. She recounted the secrets whispered by the wind, whispering secrets rustling through the leaves, the mysteries hidden within the heart of the old orchard. Jessica listened, captivated. It was as though Nana Rose's stories were a continuation of her adventure, a seamless blend of imagination and reality. She learned that no single place or time confined the magic of childhood.

As Nana Rose continued her stories, Jessica imagined that the magic wasn't about the places, but about the sense of wonder and discovery. Nana Rose did not tell orchard tales; She recounted a memorable adventure — a hidden cave concealed behind a curtain of ivy, its entrance shrouded in mystery. Nana Rose described the thrill of discovery, the excitement of exploring the unknown, and the sense of wonder that filled her as she ventured into the darkness, her heart pounding with anticipation.

Inside the cave, she had found sparkling crystals that glittered like captured starlight, reflecting the light of her small lantern. She had felt a profound connection to the earth, a deep sense of belonging. She had spent hours in that cave, creating her world, her kingdom of wonder.

Nana Rose's stories inspired Jessica to tap into her creativity and storytelling abilities. She began weaving her tales, embellishing her backyard adventures with details and descriptions inspired by Nana Rose's narratives. She learned to create rich, sensory experiences, using words to paint vivid pictures, evoke emotions, and transport her listeners to other worlds. The two spent the rest of the afternoon lost in storytelling, sharing their dreams, hopes, and adventures.

As the sun began to set, casting long shadows across the room, Nana Rose presented Jessica with a small, carved wooden box. Inside lay a collection of smooth, gray stones, each emitting a faint, warm glow. "These are stones from my secret cave," Nana Rose explained, her voice soft and full of meaning. "Each one holds a memory, a story, a piece of magic."

Jessica held the stones in her palm, sensing their warmth radiating from them. They were tangible reminders of the power of imagination, the beauty of nature, and the enduring magic of childhood adventures. They were a connection, a legacy of wonder passed from generation to generation.

The gray stones, a gift from her grandmother, became precious keepsakes, a testament to the two generations' magical journeys. They reminded us that the magic of adventure and the power of imagination transcend time and culture, uniting hearts and nurturing a passion for storytelling, nature, and endless possibilities. The whispered secrets of the willows, the grumpy gnome's fondness for raspberries, and the shimmer of the Wishing Well were now enriched with Nana Rose's tales of childhood adventures, weaving together a tapestry of intergenerational magic, a legacy of imagination passed down through time.

Chapter 23: The Neighbors' Unique Perspectives

Sensing a surge of confidence after sharing her adventures with Nana Rose, The vibrant multicultural community surrounding her home always intrigued her. There was Señora Rodriguez, with her bright smile and stories of her childhood in Mexico, filled with lush jungles and mystical creatures. Mr. Kim, quiet and observant, found beauty in simplicity; his garden bloomed with fragrant herbs and exotic flowers. And last, there was young Leo, a boisterous boy from Italy, whose imagination rivaled her own.

She first approached Señora Rodriguez, whose small house was next to a bougainvillea riot. The aroma of spiced coffee wafted from her open window, mingling with the sweet scent of the flowers. Señora Rodriguez, a woman whose eyes held the wisdom of ages, listened as Jessica recounted her adventures, her voice filled with the enthusiasm of a seasoned explorer.

"Ay, Mija," Señora Rodriguez said, her voice warm and melodious, as Jessica finished her story. "Your backyard sounds like a milagro, a miracle! It reminds me of the enchanted forests of my childhood, where the trees whispered secrets to the wind, whispering secrets, and the flowers sang songs to the stars like ancient watchers. In Mexico, we believe that every plant and creature holds a spirit and a hint of magic. Your grumpy gnome, mija, he is like the duendes of the forests, mischievous but kind." She chuckled, a warm, throaty sound. "Perhaps he needed a raspberry to appease his grumbling spirit, like we might offer a small gift to the spirits of nature to gain their favor."

Señora Rodriguez explained that in her culture, respect for nature was paramount. The world's delicate balance depended on every element, small or large. She even pointed out that certain herbs growing in her garden could soothe the skin, like the way the glowing crystals seemed to soothe Jessica's soul. "That cave, Mija," she said, her eyes twinkling. "It reminds me of the sacred caves where our ancestors would leave offerings to the gods, where the earth itself held power and mystery."

Next, Jessica visited Mr. Kim. His garden was a riot of color and scent, a testament to his quiet dedication. He spoke little, but his gentle smile and attentive gaze made Jessica comfortable. As she recounted her backyard adventures, Mr. Kim listened, his eyes twinkling with understanding. When she finished, he nodded with a serene expression.

"Balance," he murmured, his voice soft. Your backyard displays a beautiful balance, a harmony between the real and the imagined. Beauty lives everywhere, even in the ordinary, much like this tree shows. The mountains, he explained, represented strength and resilience, while the flowing streams symbolized life's constant change and renewal for her. He described the calming effect of the gentle sounds of nature and the way the wind whispering secrets rustled through the pine trees. He then explained how different cultures used various plants for food, medicine, and other daily necessities, emphasizing the importance of understanding and respecting nature.

Jessica shared her adventures with Leo. He listened with wide-eyed wonder, his imagination engaged. With his quick wit and energetic demeanor, Leo offered his interpretation of Jessica's story. He identified with the grumpy gnome, declaring that he understood grumpy. "Everyone gets grumpy sometimes," he explained. Nona says crankiness means needing pasta and a nap. With unrestrained enthusiasm, he began weaving his story into Jessica's, adding pirate battles amongst the flowerbeds, a dragon made of climbing roses, and a hidden treasure that shimmered with an untold meaning of chocolate coins in the Wishing Well.

Leo, with his vivid imagination, reinterpreted Jessica's adventure through the lens of his own experiences. He saw parallels between his backyard games and Jessica's fantastical world. Adventures among olive groves and sun-drenched vineyards filled his Italian childhood, a topic he discussed. He discussed legendary Italian folklore creatures, including mischievous folletti and protective fate. Italy's changing seasons, he explained, brought a unique magic to the landscape, with vibrant spring greens and fall golds. He even explained that his nonna's garden contained plants and herbs with mystical properties, which were used for medicinal purposes and to create charms and protective amulets.

Through these conversations, Jessica imagined her backyard was a canvas for sharing stories. The whispering willows, the grumpy gnome, and the shimmering Wishing Well took on new meanings, enriched by the diverse perspectives of her community. Señora Rodriguez's understanding of nature spirits, Mr. Kim's emphasis on harmony, and Leo's incorporation of Italian folklore created a vibrant tapestry of interpretations, revealing to her the universality of imagination and the power of diverse cultural perspectives. It was a reminder that magic, like imagination, knew no boundaries; it was a universal language that resonated with everyone, regardless of age, background, or culture. The simple act of sharing her adventures not only brought her closer to her neighbors, but also transformed her understanding of her backyard, enriching the magic that lived within. The ordinary backyard, once a private space, had become a canvas painted with the brushstrokes of imagination.

Chapter 24: Celebrating Diversity and Imagination

The sun dipped below the horizon, casting long shadows across Jessica's backyard. The warm evening air carried the sounds of crickets and rustling leaves. She sat on the porch swing, the gentle swaying motion a soothing rhythm to her thoughts. The day had been extraordinary. The simple act of sharing her adventures had blossomed into something far greater than she could have imagined.

Señora Rodriguez's words, mentioning Milagros and her spirits, occupied her thoughts. These words resonated with Jessica. The grumpy gnome, a source of minor irritation, seemed less cranky and more... whimsical. Perhaps, she mused, he was a guardian of the backyard's magic, a protector of its secrets, like the duendes Señora Rodriguez had described. The idea sparked a new level of appreciation for her fantastical world. She imagined the gnome not as a grumpy old man but as a mischievous spirit, playing tricks and guarding the hidden treasures of her magical kingdom. This new perspective added a layer of depth to her adventures, transforming the simple act of encountering the gnome into an interaction with a mystical being.

Mr. Kim's words echoed in her mind, the gentle wisdom of his "balance." She realized he was right. The disparate elements of her backyard–the sturdy oak tree, the playful butterflies, the grumpy gnome–all existed in a delicate harmony, each contributing to the overall magic. It wasn't a random collection of elements but a crafted ecosystem of wonder, where even the contradictory elements worked together in perfect balance. This realization broadened Jessica's understanding of her creative process, teaching her the importance of finding balance and harmony in her stories and the imaginative worlds they created.

Leo's infectious enthusiasm and imaginative retelling of her adventures made her laugh again. His addition to pirate battles and chocolate coin treasures was absurd, yet fitting. It reminded her that imagination knows no boundaries and that different perspectives can shape and reshape stories. It was in these differences, in these creative interpretations, that the true magic lived. From his perspective, brimming with Italian folklore and a zest for life, Leo added a vibrant layer to the tapestry of her backyard's narrative.

Jessica recognized the common threads that connected their cultures: a reverence for nature, a belief in hidden magic, and the power of storytelling. Señora Rodriguez's Mexican heritage, Mr. Kim's Korean background, and Leo's Italian roots all contributed. It wasn't a collection of diverse viewpoints but a harmonious blend of cultures, with each element enriching a more meaningful tapestry of understanding.

That night, Jessica dreamed of a vibrant world where her backyard blended with the landscapes of Mexico, Korea, and Italy. Bougainvillea intertwined with cherry blossoms and olive trees, forming a lush, fantastical garden. Butterflies with wings, the colors of the Italian flag, flitted among the flowers. It was a beautiful chaos, a kaleidoscope of cultures and landscapes, all united by the common thread of imagination.

The next day, armed with newfound insights, Jessica expanded her backyard adventures. At the base of the oak tree, she built a small shrine, leaving small offerings of berries and wildflowers as a tribute to Señora Rodriguez's teachings about respecting nature. Near the wishing well, she arranged smooth stones, crafting a miniature Zen garden inspired by Mr. Kim's emphasis on balance. Honoring Leo's storytelling and the charm of Italian folklore, she added a small, carved wooden gnome to her collection.

Her expanded backyard became a vibrant reflection of her broadening worldview. The whimsical creatures–from talking butterflies to a family of mischievous squirrels—appeared even more lively, their playful antics enriched by the diverse cultural perspectives she had encountered. The glowing crystals in the cave shimmered with an even brighter light, their magical aura enhanced by her understanding of the sacred caves of Señora Rodriguez's ancestors. Even the grumpy gnome seemed less irritable, his presence now adding a playful mystery rather than mere annoyance.

The stories she created now flowed with a newfound richness. She wrote the gnome's journey, from a grumpy old fellow, inspired by Señora Rodriguez's tales of nature spirits. She wrote about the careful balance between the oak tree's strength and the butterflies', echoing Mr. Kim's emphasis on harmony. Her story describes the mischievous adventures of a band of folletti who teamed up with her pet hamster, resulting in a tale rich with Italian folklore.

Jessica imagined that her experiences or cultural background didn't limit her imagination. The limitless space contained global richness and diversity. She could draw inspiration from anywhere, from anyone. Her backyard wasn't her private playground; it was a meeting place, a space where different cultures and perspectives could come together, creating a unique and vibrant tapestry of wonder.

She organized a "Backyard Festival" to share her expanded world with her neighbors and friends. She invited everyone to bring their favorite foods, stories, and games. Señora Rodriguez brought traditional Mexican pastries. Mr. Kim brought fragrant teas and showed the children how to create miniature bonsai trees. Leo told tales of Italian folktales and mischievous sprites. Children from all backgrounds came, sharing their creative expressions and interpretations of magic. They crafted miniature gnomes, painted fantastical landscapes, and shared stories filled with vibrant creatures and whimsical adventures. The festival developed into a lively celebration of imagination and diversity. It was a testament to the power of sharing warmly, weaving their stories into her world experiences, the joy of discovering common ground despite different cultural backgrounds. It showed how imagination, like nature itself, could transcend boundaries, fostering a sense of belonging and unity.

Through it all, Jessica's backyard remained her primary source of inspiration, her playground for creating stories and celebrating her unique blend of cultural influences. The oak tree, once a tree, now stood as a symbol of resilience; the flowerbeds were more than plants; they were a canvas for cross-cultural stories and collaborative creative expression; and the grumpy gnome, once a symbol of irritation, became a whimsical emblem of the unexpected joy of diverse perspectives and embracing differences.

Jessica learned that the most magical places are those where imagination and community intertwine, where differences are celebrated. Jessica's once-simple backyard transformed into a powerful symbol of imagination's universal language, reminding everyone that wonder knows no boundaries and that magic exists anywhere, even in familiar places, if one sees it. The mundane became extraordinary, all thanks to the power of a vibrant, diverse community. Her journey was not a personal adventure, but a shared warmth, weaving their stories into her world expedition, into the boundless realms of imagination, fueled by the common thread of creativity that connected them all. The backyard festival became an annual tradition.

Chapter 25: Embracing the Power of Community

The days following the initial backyard explorations were a blur of activity. Jessica revisited her enchanted world, each visit revealing new layers of wonder. The talking butterflies, once whimsical additions, now seemed to whisper secrets. Señora Rodriguez's tales of Milagros imbued the glowing crystals in the cave with a more profound significance, transforming them from beautiful rocks to powerful symbols of hidden magic. Mr. Kim's emphasis on balance created the delicate ecosystem in the backyard, where even the grumpy gnome seemed to play a crucial role in maintaining the harmony of the miniature world. Leo's infectious energy infused the entire space with a playful spirit, adding a layer of joyful absurdity to the fantastical landscape.

One afternoon, while sketching a flamboyant butterfly in her notebook, Jessica imagined the impact of sharing her discoveries. It wasn't the individual stories that were amplified; instead, it was the sharing that amplified the magic. Her grandmother, a keen storyteller herself, had often said that stories gain strength with each retelling, each new ear they reach. It was as if sharing added another enchantment, enriching the experience for everyone involved.

This realization led Jessica to invite her school friends to visit her enchanted backyard. Hesitant, the magic Jessica created soon captivated her friends. They brought their imaginative interpretations to the scene, contributing to the ever-evolving narrative. One friend, Maya, envisioned the swing set as a time-traveling machine, sending them on adventures to ancient Egypt. Another, David, transformed the willow trees into mystical guardians, each whispering a cryptic puzzle that tested both heart and minds and prophecies.

The collaborative storytelling was exhilarating. Jessica, no longer the sole creator, collaborated on epic quests, whimsical games, and fantastical creatures. Each child brought their unique experiences and perspectives, enriching the collective imagination. The grumpy gnome, a source of amusement, became a mischievous participant, leading them on a treasure hunt and leaving cryptic clues.

The collaboration wasn't limited to games and stories. Inspired by Señora Rodriguez's stories of Mexican folk art, Jessica's friends helped her decorate the base of the oak tree with colorful painted stones and small handcrafted figurines. They even created miniature versions of the traditional alebrijes, vibrant creatures born from the imagination of Mexican artisans. Mr. Kim, ever practical, helped them make small, sustainable gardens near the flower beds, teaching them the importance of caring for nature and respecting the delicate balance of the ecosystem.

True to his Italian heritage, Leo introduced them to the concept of folletti, mischievous sprites who lived in the garden and played playful tricks on those who dared to enter their domain. He even taught them a traditional Italian song about these magical creatures, which they sang as they wandered through the whispering willows along the make-believe river. The collaboration enhanced the existing elements, adding new textures and depth to the vibrant landscape.

This creativity expanded beyond the physical realm. Jessica and her friends started a collaborative storytelling project, writing short stories about the adventures in their enchanted backyard. A different person wrote each chapter, weaving their styles and imaginations together. The result was an imaginative collection of narratives, a testament to the power of collaborative storytelling. The Grumpy Gnome became a recurring character, with his interactions varying based on each author's interpretation. Sometimes, he was a benevolent guide; other times, a mischievous trickster. The oak tree served as a majestic landmark and a source of wisdom, its leaves whispering secrets to those who listened. The ordinary becomes extraordinary through the power of collective imagination.

One evening, as the sun cast a golden hue across the backyard, Jessica's mother joined the group, captivated by the children's stories. Her stories added a dimension to the narrative, bridging the gap between generations and highlighting the continuity of imagination across time.

Jessica's grandmother, known for her intricate storytelling, added complexity to the narrative, weaving in ancient legends and folklore. She connected the children's whimsical adventures to the rich tapestry of human storytelling, reminding them that the power of imagination transcended cultures and time.

Her tales added depth and significance to the already fantastical world. She discussed mythical creatures from different cultures, explaining how similar creatures existed in different folklore traditions. This underscored the universal appeal to imagination, the innate human desire to create stories, and magic.

Stories did not create a magical world; they fostered a profound sense of community. The children became close friends, united by their love for adventure and creativity. They learned to appreciate each other's perspectives, celebrating their differences and discovering the richness and diversity that their collaborative world brought. The sense of camaraderie extended beyond the children. Jessica's family, neighbors, and friends all felt part of the unfolding adventure, creating a web of interconnectedness and her world experience.

The power of the community extended even further. News of Jessica's enchanted backyard spread throughout the neighborhood, attracting new friends and visitors. People from different backgrounds brought unique stories and perspectives, enriching the collective imagination. A retired librarian told stories of fantastical creatures.

This expansion of the community deepened the backyard's enchantment. The stories became more prosperous, complex, and inclusive, reflecting the diverse perspectives that enriched the collective narrative. Sharing stories transformed the backyard into a hub of creativity. In this meeting place, imaginations collided, and friendships blossomed. Jessica uncovered that true magic was not in the fantastical world she had created but also in the community it had inspired.

The experience underscored the value of embracing differences and recognizing each person's unique contributions. It showed that imagination knows no boundaries, that creativity thrives in collaboration, and that the most magical experiences are often those with others. The community extended beyond the physical space of the backyard. The woven stories formed a rich tapestry, reflecting the diverse backgrounds and experiences of the individuals involved.

Jessica's enchanted backyard became a testament to the power of sharing warmly, weaving their stories into her world imagination, a vibrant symbol of the magic that unfolds when people come together to create and celebrate. It was a space where the ordinary transformed into the extraordinary, where individual stories intertwined to form a collective narrative, and a sense of community and belonging grew stronger with each story. It was a lesson in the transformative power of community, a celebration of imagination.

Chapter 26: Making a Wish at the Wishing Well

As Jessica approached the wishing well, the air hung heavy with the scent of honeysuckle and damp earth. It was not grand or ornate, like the ones she had seen in fairy tales. Instead, it was a simple, rustic structure, half-hidden beneath the weeping willow's cascading branches. The ancient and wise willow seemed to guard the well, its leaves whispering secrets to the gentle breeze. Rough-hewn stones, with moss clinging to their uneven surface like a verdant tapestry, formed the well. A weathered wooden bucket, its rope frayed and worn, hung beside the opening, inviting her to cast her wish into the depths.

Jessica kneeled beside the well, the cool earth grounding her. The water shimmered, reflecting the dappled sunlight that filtered through the leaves and created an ethereal glow. She was not sure what to wish. Material things felt insignificant compared to the wonder she'd already experienced. She already had her enchanted backyard, a world of magic and adventure. What more could she desire?

There was a thoughtful pause. Her friends, family, and supportive community already embraced her whimsical world. Yet, a longing stirred within her. It was not a selfish wish for more toys or candy. This was deeper. It was a yearning for the magic to continue, deepen, grow, and share. She wished her adventures would never end, her imagination would remain vibrant and boundless, and she could share her world with those who wanted to see it.

With a deep breath, Jessica cupped her hands, whispering her wish into the well's depths. The words felt weightless yet profound, carrying her hopes and dreams into the heart of the earth. As her wish echoed in the stillness, a single drop of water splashed from the well's surface, catching the sunlight and sparkling like a tiny diamond. It was as if the well had responded, acknowledging her wish and approving its purity.

A sense of peace washed over her. It surpassed a simple wish fulfillment; it felt meaningful, a validation, a perfect alignment with her ambitions. The whispering willows seemed to sway in agreement, their rustling leaves sounding like a gentle chorus of approval. The air, already fragrant with honeysuckle, was now infused with magic, palpable and real. Jessica smiled, knowing she wouldn't receive a literal, tangible fulfillment of her wish. It was a wish to preserve and expand something already miraculous: her imagination and the ability to share its fruits.

As she stood, she noticed something she had not seen before. A small, carved wooden bird, perched on the edge of the well, glowed. It was unlike anything she had ever seen — a whimsical blend of several birds, each element enhancing the beauty and mystery of the others. It looked like a small hummingbird crossed with a majestic phoenix; the colors were vibrant against the gray stone. The bird seemed to pulse with a soft, inner glow.

Curiosity piqued; Jessica picked up the little bird. It felt warm to the touch, its smooth wood radiating a gentle energy. The bird whispered, "Follow the moonbeams," as she held it. Intrigued, Jessica looked up at the sky. The moon, a sliver of silver in the twilight, cast long, silvery beams across the garden. Following the moon's path, she navigated through her enchanted backyard. The moonbeams guided her, illuminating hidden paths and unseen wonders. The ordinary transformed into the extraordinary under the moon's silvery glow. A shimmering garden of luminous blossoms replaced the familiar flower beds, each petal glowing with an otherworldly light. The oak tree, imposing, transformed into a majestic silhouette against the moonlit sky, its branches reaching towards the stars like ancient watchers.

The moonbeams led her to a clearing she had never noticed before. In the center stood a shimmering pool of water, reflecting the moon like a perfect mirror. The water was alive with bioluminescent creatures, tiny lights dancing and weaving intricate patterns in the darkness. The air hummed with an almost imperceptible energy, a symphony of unseen magic. Jessica approached the pool, her heart filled with awe.

As she gazed into the water, she saw reflected in it her physical form, her inner self, and her vibrant imagination. She saw herself as a storyteller, weaving tales of wonder that inspired them with her creativity. It was a powerful and moving image, a vision that confirmed the path she was on.

She noticed that the moon's reflection was not static. It pulsed with a gentle rhythm, morphing into fleeting images: a majestic griffin soaring across a moonlit sky, a group of children playing in a sun-dappled forest, a friendly gnome tending to a magical garden. Each image was a glimpse of a potential future adventure, a testament to the boundless possibilities held within her imagination. The visions confirmed her immense creative power.

The little wooden bird in her hand glowed brighter, pulsing. It felt as though it was radiating energy, warmth, and possibility. The bird seemed alive and reacting to the magical energy around it and Jessica's wish. With newfound courage, Jessica whispered, "I'm ready for more adventures." The glow intensified, and a tiny, sparkling dust settled over Jessica, caressing her skin. The effect increased her energy and confidence.

She left the pool of moonlight, walking on the moonlit path back toward her home. The little wooden bird now seemed to hold a deeper meaning for her, a symbolic reminder of her magic, the adventures that awaited her, and the importance of sharing the wonder with others. As the moon cast its silvery glow over her, Jessica knew that her wish had come true. Her adventures would continue, not in her backyard, but in her mind and the hearts of all those with whom she shared her magic. Her capacity to create stories would grow, and her desire to share the magic with others would provide many new experiences.

Recent adventures filled the following days, fueled by her renewed sense of purpose and deepened understanding of the magic in her imagination and the power of sharing it. She continued to weave stories with her friends, adding new characters, expanding the boundaries of their enchanted world, and creating deeper bonds of friendship. The grumpy gnome developed into a more nuanced character, capable of both mischievous and surprising acts of kindness. The talking butterflies revealed more of the garden's secrets, leading Jessica and her friends on quests that combined imagination and real-world learning.

Her collaboration with her neighbors deepened, adding additional elements to the fabric of her enchanted world. Señora Rodriguez introduced them to traditional Mexican storytelling techniques, while Mr. Kim's practical insights helped them create sustainable aspects within their imaginary space. Leo's infectious enthusiasm continued to inspire additional levels of creativity, enriching their adventures with a hearty dose of humor and fun.

The wishing well became a recurring symbol, a reminder of Jessica's wish, her unwavering belief in the power of her imagination, and the limitless possibilities of friendship, collaboration, and creativity. Jessica's wish found its answer, not in material things, but in a deeper understanding of her potential and imagination, which enabled her to create stories and forge meaningful connections. This connection formed the basis of her growing magic, extending beyond her backyard into the community and the hearts of everyone she touched with her stories. The most extraordinary magic, she realized, lay not in her creation of a magical world, but in the community her magic inspired.

Chapter 27: The Wells Response and a New Riddle

The sparkling water droplet wasn't the well's sole reply. As Jessica reached to pick up the carved wooden bird, a faint tremor ran through the ground, subtle enough almost to be missed. The well seemed to sigh, a low rumble emanating from the depths. Then, nestled among the moss at the base of the well, she spotted it: a smooth, gray stone, almost perfectly round, resting on a bed of velvety green moss. Its surface displayed a new cryptic puzzle that tested both heart and mind, its script shimmering.

Jessica easily deciphered the elegant yet straightforward words. They spoke of "a place where shadows dance and sunlight sleeps," hidden "behind the laughter of the willow, beneath the gaze of the silent oak." The cryptic puzzle that tested both heart and mind was intriguing, leaving Jessica with a sense of exciting anticipation. Where was this place? What secrets did it hold?

She felt the small wooden bird, warm within her grasp, thrumming; Jessica felt a surge of excitement. The magic was not fading; it was intensifying, leading her on a new adventure. The whispers of the willows seemed to urge her forward, their rustling leaves sounding like a playful invitation. The cryptic puzzle that tested both heart and mind was a trial with hidden stakes, a playful game of hide-and-seek within the familiar landscape of her enchanted backyard. It was a key to unlock an additional layer of magic, an alternative path into the extraordinary world she had created.

She examined the cryptic puzzle that tested both heart and mind again, turning the smooth stone in her hand. The words were almost hypnotic, their subtle glow a promise of discovery. "Shadows dance and sunlight sleeps..." What could it mean? Sunlight bathed the oak tree, but the willows' weeping branches created pockets of shadow. Could the hidden place be somewhere within the willow's shade?

Jessica ventured towards the weeping willow, its branches draping down like a green curtain. The air beneath the willow was cooler, a welcome contrast to the afternoon sun. She parted the branches, peering into the depths of the willow's embrace. It wanted to enter a secret grotto, a place untouched by the brightness of day. The air was vibrant with the gentle rustle of leaves, while sunlight streamed through the foliage in dappled patterns, forming a dance of light and shadow that mirrored the enigmatic puzzle challenging both heart and mind's words.

She remembered the cryptic puzzle that tested both heart and mind, mentioning the "silent oak," implying a contrast to the whispering willow. She looked towards the mighty oak tree, its branches stretching like strong, silent arms towards the sky. The oak seemed to watch over her, a comforting reminder of stability amidst the unfolding mystery. Intricate ground patterns, woven from willow shadows, reflected the stone's words.

Following the pattern of shadows, Jessica traced a path beneath the willows' weeping branches. The ground felt softer here, covered in a thick layer of moss and decaying leaves. She noticed a slight dip in the ground, almost imperceptible at first glance. Could this be it? The hidden place where shadows danced and sunlight slept? With growing excitement, Jessica kneeled and brushed away the leaves. She uncovered a small opening hidden beneath the willow's roots. It was a narrow passage, large enough to crawl through—the air from within felt cool and damp, carrying a hint of something mysterious.

Jessica squeezed through the opening. Long, the passage led her deeper into the earth. As she descended, the air grew colder, the occasional drip of water breaking the silence that echoed in the growing darkness. Only the faint glow of phosphorescent moss broke the darkness clinging to the passage walls. The passage opened into a small cavern. A calm and damp, yet fresh air enveloped the area, carrying with it the scent of earth and something sweet. Lining the circular cavern's walls were glistening crystals, radiating a soft, ethereal glow. The light was reminiscent of the moonlit pool she had uncovered earlier. The crystals reflected the light, creating an enchanting, magical ambiance.

A small, crystal-clear pool of water was in the cavern's center, nestled amongst the crystals. A breathtaking, mesmerizing sight was created as the still water reflected the crystalline walls and glowing crystals. The water shimmered with a faint, internal light. The cavern glowed, a breathtaking and unimaginable sight.

A sense of peace settled over Jessica as she stared into the reflection. This place, despite being open, felt like a magical, peaceful sanctuary. The cryptic puzzle that tested both heart and mind had led her to a secret, beautiful world hidden beneath the surface of her backyard. This hidden realm, though unlike ours, possessed an ancient mystique despite its connection to the surface. It extended the world she had already created, a deeper exploration of her imagination.

As she sat by the pool, the wooden bird in her hand pulsed with a gentle light, echoing the subtle luminescence of the cavern. She felt a sense of completion, having uncovered a vital piece of her enchanted world. The cryptic puzzle that tested both heart and mind had not led her to a physical location, but to a deeper understanding of the limitless potential within her imagination. A faint melody drifted through the air, almost too subtle to perceive. It was a melody of crystalline chimes, each note pure and clear, echoing through the cavern. As the melody unfolded, a vision flickered in her mind: a vibrant, colorful bird, unlike any she had ever seen, singing the same melody she could now hear.

It was a bird woven from moonlight and starlight, its feathers shimmering with a thousand hues. The vision faded, but the melody continued, guiding, inspiring, and encouraging her to explore this uncovered landscape. The cavern's magic was not visual. It permeated her senses, awakening a new creative spark within her. Ideas flowed like the crystals were whispering stories, inspiring new characters, and painting vivid scenes in her mind.

The melody intensified, and the images became sharper and more distinct. She saw a scene of mischievous sprites dancing amongst the crystals, a wise old owl perched on a crystal, and a picture of a miniature waterfall cascading from a fissure in the cavern wall. Clear and vibrant, the images portrayed stories waiting to be told and adventures waiting to unfold.

She picked up a smooth, gray stone from the pool's edge, similar to the one bearing the cryptic puzzle that tested both heart and mind. The stone glowed as she held it, and a new image formed in her mind. It was a picture of a hidden path winding through the crystals, leading to a chamber beyond. The image faded, leaving her to continue her discovery of further adventures within this realm. The cavern functioned less than a destination and more than a portal; countless adventures awaited, her vision made manifest, creativity boundless. The whispering willows, the silent oak, and now the magical cavern played their part in the ever-expanding tapestry of her incredible world.

Chapter 28: Following the New Clues

The melody of crystalline chimes faded, leaving a lingering sweetness in the air. Still captivated by the cavern's beauty, Jessica rose. Now, cool, the smooth gray stone felt significant in her hand. The cryptic puzzle that tested both heart and mind's answer unveiled a stunning location; her journey continued, rather than concluding. The path ahead, both literal and metaphorical, beckoned her forward.

She traced the edge of the crystal-clear pool, her fingers brushing against the cool, smooth surface. Despite its stillness, the water seemed to pulse with a subtle energy, a vibrant life force resonating with the luminous crystals surrounding it. She imagined tiny creatures, perhaps no bigger than her thumbnail, swimming unseen within the depths, their lives as magical and wondrous as the cavern itself. She pictured them shimmering, their movements creating ripples that would disturb the perfect reflection of the crystal walls. That thought enhanced the already magical backyard, revealing a hidden world.

A subtle hum, a resonant vibration from the crystals, filled the air of the cavern. It was a comforting hum, a sense of ancient power and deep-seated magic, a sensation that resonated deep within Jessica's heart. She felt an overwhelming sense of connection to this hidden world, a connection that transcended the simple exploration of a physical space. This was not about discovery; it was about understanding the power of her imagination and the boundless nature of the world she had created.

The new stone, still warm in her hand, pulsed, its warmth a comforting counterpoint to the cavern's coolness. The puzzle, taxing both intellect and spirit, underscored her determination, foreshadowing more adventures. This cryptic puzzle, a test of mind and spirit, yielded no hidden place.

Following the faint image of the glowing stone, Jessica explored the cavern's perimeter. The crystals varied in size and shape, some clustering in dense formations, while others stood alone like solitary sentinels. Their luminescence also varied; some glowed with a soft, milky white light, others radiated a vibrant, amethyst hue, and others emitted a gentle, emerald green glow. The diversity of the crystals added to the cavern's enchanting ambiance, making it a unique and wondrous place.

She uncovered a small fissure in the cavern wall, noticeable amidst the crystalline formations. From the fissure, a tiny stream of water trickled down, creating a miniature waterfall that cascaded into the crystal-clear pool. A faint whisper heightened the cavern's serene atmosphere. The water, pure and clear, seemed to sparkle with an inner light, mirroring the radiance of the crystals.

As she continued her exploration, she found the hidden path the stone had revealed. A narrow, winding passage, wider than her shoulders, weaved through the crystalline formations. Throughout the cavern, a gentle hum pulsed along the path. The path felt alive, leading her into this enchanting realm.

A smaller chamber lay beyond the passage. This chamber surpassed the main cavern in magic. Phosphorescent fungi, glowing with an ethereal light, filled it. The fungi varied in size and shape, with some resembling delicate flowers and others resembling bizarre, alien-like creatures. They illuminated the chamber with a myriad of colors, creating a kaleidoscopic effect that was both enchanting and awe-inspiring.

A small crystal pedestal was in the center of the smaller chamber, nestled amongst the glowing fungi. A small carved wooden box was resting on the pedestal. The dark, rich wood formed the box, and someone had polished its surface to a high sheen. Intricate carvings adorned its sides, depicting scenes of fantastical creatures and magical landscapes. The carvings, illuminated by the fungi, shimmered as if breathing.

Jessica reached out and opened the box. A shimmering feather lay inside, nestled on a soft velvet bed. The feather was unlike anything she had ever seen. It was long and slender, its surface shimmering with a thousand colors. It felt warm and light to the touch, almost weightless. As she held it, she felt a surge of energy coursing through her veins.

The feather seemed to pulse with a gentle light, mirroring the glowing fungi surrounding her. A sharper, clearer vision emerged than in previous ones. She saw a majestic bird, its wings spanning the width of the cavern, soaring through the night sky, its feathers shimmering like a thousand stars. A powerful melody, a majestic song that resonated with the crystal's humming and the fungi's gentle whisper, accompanied the vision.

The vision faded, but the melody lingered, a vibrant echo in the chamber's silence. Jessica imagined this was no ordinary feather; it was a key, a conduit to a higher level of magic, a gateway to even more profound adventures within her enchanted backyard. The feather, box, and chamber were all part of an interconnected narrative, a story waiting to be uncovered. This discovery proved essential to her. This was not about finding hidden places; it was about unlocking her creative potential and expanding the boundaries of her fantastical world.

She closed the box, returning it to the pedestal, starting a new journey. The journey within her enchanted backyard was far from over. Each discovery led to further mysteries, adventures, and a deeper understanding of the boundless potential of her imagination. As she left the chamber, she carried the stone and the sense of wonder, ready to face whatever new challenges and discoveries awaited her in the heart of her magical realm.

The whispers of the willows, the silent gaze of the oak, and the shimmering crystals of the cavern all seemed to conspire together, inviting her further into her extraordinary world, her enchanted backyard, where adventure knew no bounds and imagination reigned supreme.

Chapter 29: Uncovering a Secret Garden

The path, illuminated by the ethereal glow of the feather, led Jessica out of the crystalline cavern and back into the familiar, yet transformed, landscape of her backyard. The air now hummed with a quieter energy, a gentler vibration that seemed to emanate from the earth beneath her feet. She clutched the smooth, gray stone and the small wooden box containing the shimmering feather, sensing the weight of their magical significance. Her journey's end remained distant; she sensed this. The whispers of the willows seemed to urge her onward, promising further wonders yet to be uncovered.

Following an almost imperceptible shift in the surrounding energy, Jessica noticed a dense thicket of bushes, unnoticed in her many explorations. They were tall and lush, their leaves a deep emerald green, almost luminous in the dappled sunlight filtering through the branches of the oak tree-mountain. An unfamiliar scent, a blend of sweet blossoms and earthy musk, wafted from within, enticing her to investigate.

She pushed aside the thick branches, her hands brushing against velvety leaves that felt soft. As she parted the foliage, a breathtaking sight unfolded before her: a secret garden, hidden from plain view, bathed in a soft, diffused light. It was as if she had stepped through a veil into another dimension, a hidden sanctuary tucked away within the familiar confines of her backyard.

The garden was a riot of color and fragrance. Flowers of every imaginable hue bloomed in profusion–vibrant reds, passionate oranges, soothing blues, and delicate pinks. There were flowers she recognized from her grandmother's garden–roses, lilies, and daisies–but they were larger, more vibrant, and more intensely fragrant than any she had ever seen before. And then there were flowers she had never seen, of impossible shapes and colors, their petals shimmering with an iridescent glow. Some resembled delicate glass sculptures, others resembled miniature works of art, their intricate designs a testament to nature's artistry. Towering over the flowerbeds were plants she could not identify, their leaves as large as dinner plates, their stems thick as her arm.

Their leaves glistened with a subtle dew, catching the light and scattering it in a dazzling display. The air thrummed with the sound of unseen insects, their buzz a gentle symphony that blended with the rustling of the leaves and the gentle whisper of the breeze. Butterflies, larger and more brightly colored than any she had encountered, fluttered among the blossoms, their wings a kaleidoscope of vibrant patterns. They seemed to dance in the air, their movements graceful and ethereal, their presence adding to the garden's enchantment.

A small, winding path, visible beneath the profusion of blossoms, beckoned Jessica deeper into the heart of the garden. As she walked along the route, she noticed that the ground beneath her feet was soft and yielding, like a thick carpet of moss. Blossoms, exotic spices, and damp soil filled the air with sweet, intoxicating, and earthy aromas. The overall effect was calming, creating a sense of peace and tranquility that washed over her.

As she ventured deeper, she uncovered a small, crystal-clear stream that meandered through the garden, its waters sparkling like a thousand tiny diamonds. The stream flowed over smooth, moss-covered stones, creating a soothing melody for the garden's serene atmosphere. Small, colorful fish darted through the clear water, their scales shimmering like jewels. Dragonflies, their wings like stained glass windows, hovered above the water's surface, their delicate bodies a testament to nature's elegance.

Along the banks of the stream, she found strange plants–luminous mushrooms that glowed with a soft, internal light ferns with leaves as fine as silk, and flowering vines that twined around ancient-looking trees, their blossoms resembling tiny bells. The trees were unlike any she had ever seen, their bark smooth and silvery, their branches reaching towards the sky like outstretched arms. They seemed ancient and wise, their presence adding to the garden's mystical charm.

Hidden amongst the trees, she uncovered a small clearing. In the center of the clearing was a willow tree, its branches weeping towards the ground, their leaves rustling in the breeze. Underneath the willow tree, nestled amongst its roots, was a small, moss-covered stone. The stone felt cool and smooth, pulsating with a gentle energy. As she touched it, a vision flashed in her mind–a picture of a hidden spring bubbling up from deep within the earth.

Following her vision, she found the hidden spring with crystal clear and sparkling water. The water tasted pure and sweet, refreshing. She drank, feeling the energy of the water coursing through her veins. She felt a kinship with garden, earth, and nature while drinking. It was a sense of belonging.

The garden offered more than beauty; It reflected Jessica's vibrant imagination, a testament to the magic she had created in her backyard. This secret garden, tucked away behind a thicket of bushes, was a treasure beyond compare — a sanctuary where she could lose herself in the beauty and wonder of nature. She could return to it, a place that would continue to inspire, trial with hidden stakes, and nurture her growing sense of wonder. This experience solidified her understanding that magic exists everywhere in her world, woven into its fabric, waiting for those with open eyes and hearts to discover it, not just in the wishing well or crystalline cave.

The sun dipped below the horizon, casting long shadows across the garden. The air grew cooler, the sounds of the insects fading into a gentle hum. Jessica knew it was time to leave, but the memory of the garden-the scent of its flowers, the feel of its cool earth beneath her feet—would remain with her long after she had returned to the familiar landscape of her backyard. The secret garden promised even greater adventures, more profound mysteries, and untold wonders. It was a reminder that even the most ordinary places can hold extraordinary secrets, and that their most incredible adventures often lie beyond the familiar. Each discovery seemed to unlock an additional layer of magic, a new pathway leading to further exploration and wonder.

Chapter 30: The Secret Garden's Inhabitants

The path continued deeper into the secret garden, winding between towering plants whose leaves shimmered with an almost ethereal glow. The air hummed with a low, resonant thrum, a sound that vibrated not in Jessica's ears but seemed to resonate within her bones. She passed luminous mushrooms, their caps pulsing with a gentle, internal light that cast an otherworldly glow upon the surrounding foliage. Some were a soft, pearly white, while others were a vibrant, almost electric blue; their stems were thick and fleshy, resembling tiny, glowing sculptures. Jessica reached to touch one, her fingertip brushing against a smooth surface. It felt alive, pulsating with a subtle energy that sent a tiny thrill up her arm.

Further on, she uncovered a colony of ants unlike any she had ever seen. Their bodies were enormous, iridescent green and black, marching in disciplined lines along the mossy ground. They carried tiny, glittering crystals, larger than themselves, each reflecting the light in a dazzling display. Jessica watched, mesmerized, as they transported their treasures, their movements precise and coordinated, a tiny army on a grand mission. She wondered about their destination, the purpose of their tireless work, adding a layer of mystery to the already enchanting garden.

She came across a patch of carnivorous plants, their delicate, Flower-like blossoms concealing menacing traps. The plants were unlike anything she had ever seen in books or documentaries; their vibrant colors were a deceptive mask for their predatory nature. She could almost hear the faintest click of their traps snapping shut, a sound that was both intriguing and unsettling, a reminder that even in the most beautiful places, danger could lurk. She kept a respectful distance, fascinated by their intricate mechanisms, a marvel of nature's design.

Among the more familiar plants, interspersed with the exotic flora, Jessica uncovered a patch of her grandmother's favorite roses, unlike any she had ever seen before. Their petals were a deep, velvety crimson, exuding an intoxicating fragrance that filled the air. They seemed to glow with an inner light, their beauty almost overwhelming. She touched a petal feeling the soft texture and the lingering scent, a bittersweet reminder of her grandmother and her love for the garden.

The path led her to a clearing dominated by a giant, ancient oak, its branches draped with shimmering, silver moss that hung like curtains of moonlight. Ancient wisdom infused the ozone-heavy air below the oak. Jessica experienced profound awe and reverence before something old and powerful.

She noticed the ancient symbols carved on the tree trunk, which radiated a subtle energy. Although indecipherable, these symbols communicated with her on a deeper, intuitive level. A small, carved wooden box sat at the base of the oak. Someone made the box from dark, polished wood; its surface was smooth. She opened it. A perfect acorn was inside, nestled on a soft velvet bed. The acorn seemed to glow, emitting a warm, golden light that filled the box. A faint energy pulsed through her hand as she picked it up, warmth and comfort enveloping her. She closed the box, feeling a sense of wonder and anticipation for what secrets this small, unassuming acorn might hold.

As she continued her exploration, Jessica stumbled upon a hidden waterfall cascading over moss-covered rocks into a crystal-clear pool. The water sparkled and shimmered, reflecting the sunlight in a dazzling display. The sound of rushing water, a soothing symphony that calmed her senses, filled the air around the waterfall. Small colored fish darted in and out of the pool, their movements graceful. Dragonflies, their wings like stained glass, danced in the air, their delicate bodies a testament to nature's intricate beauty.

Along the banks of the pool, Jessica uncovered several unusual plants that seemed to absorb and refract light in extraordinary ways. Some glowed with an internal luminescence, while others shimmered with iridescent colors that shifted and changed depending on the angle of the light. She spent a long time observing these remarkable specimens, marveling at their unique properties and feeling a deep connection to their delicate beauty. It was as if the plants were communicating with her, whispering secrets of the earth and the hidden magic within.

Butterflies with wings like stained glass landed on her outstretched hand, their delicate bodies strong and sturdy. A tiny, iridescent beetle crawled onto her arm, its shell reflecting the rainbow of colors surrounding it. She felt a profound connection with these creatures, an understanding that transcended the boundaries between human and nature. It was a feeling of mutual respect and harmony.

As the sun set, casting long shadows across the garden, Jessica felt a sense of sadness, knowing she had to return home. She felt a wordless connection to the garden's beauty. She understood the importance of preserving this hidden sanctuary, protecting its unique beauty and delicate ecosystem from the dangers that threatened the natural world outside. It was a responsibility she felt, a commitment she made to herself and to the enchanting garden.

As she left the secret garden, stepping back through the concealing thicket of bushes, she carried a renewed sense of wonder and responsibility. The garden was a reminder of nature's incredible resilience and beauty, a testament to the interconnectedness of all living things, and a profound inspiration for her future adventures within her enchanted backyard. She was no longer a girl playing in her backyard; she was an explorer in a world of her creation, filled with wonder, magic, and endless possibilities.

Chapter 31: Exploring the Discovered Area

The path, visible now, wound through a dense thicket of ferns, their fronds unfurling like emerald ribbons. The air grew cooler and damper, and the scent of pine needles, sharp and invigorating, mingled with the rich, earthy smell of damp soil. Jessica pushed aside a curtain of hanging moss, revealing a breathtaking sight. Before her lay a grove of ancient trees, their gnarled branches intertwined like the fingers of giants, creating a magical, secluded space, bathed in a soft, filtered light.

Sunlight, dappled and diffused by the dense canopy above, painted the forest floor in shifting patterns of light and shadow. The trees were breathtaking, majestic giants reaching for the sky. Moss, dense and velvety, draped some, hanging in curtains of emerald green.

The air in the grove contained a slight energy. It was a soundless symphony, a deep resonance that vibrated in Jessica's chest, filling her with peace and wonder. She felt an inexplicable connection to this place, as if she had known it all along. It was as if the trees whispered secrets, ancient stories etched into their being.

Jessica walked into the grove and saw a small stream with clear, flowing water between the tree roots. The stream gurgled, its melody a soothing counterpoint to the hushed whispers of the forest. The water was so clear that she could see the smooth, rounded pebbles at the bottom, their colors a kaleidoscope of browns, grays, and whites. Tiny silver fish darted between the stones, their movements quick and fluid, their scales reflecting the light in a dazzling display.

Along the banks of the stream, vibrant wildflowers grew in profusion. Their petals were a symphony of colors—deep blues, fiery oranges, soft pinks, and dazzling yellows—a lively contrast to the muted greens and browns of the forest floor. Some flowers she recognized, others new, their shapes and colors alien and intriguing. She bent down to examine a cluster of blossoms, their velvety-soft petals and intoxicating fragrance.

A flash of iridescent blue caught her eye. A hummingbird with emerald green, sapphire blue, and ruby red plumage hovered before bright orange flowers. It zipped from blossom to blossom, its movements so rapid that they were challenging to follow, a blur of color against the green background. Jessica watched in fascination, mesmerized by its incredible speed and agility. It was a tiny jewel of nature's artistry.

Further, Jessica uncovered a clearing bathed in a soft, ethereal light, and in the center of the clearing stood a towering tree, older and larger than any she had seen. Its trunk was so thick that it would take several children to wrap their arms around it, and its branches spread wide, creating a dense, leafy canopy of shade. The bark had intricate carvings, ancient symbols humming with quiet energy.

She approached the tree, her hands resting on its rough bark. The pleasant chill washed over her, bringing serenity. The carvings seemed to pulse with a subtle light, and she felt an inexplicable connection to the tree, a sense of ancient wisdom and profound understanding. She ran her fingers over the intricate designs, feeling their texture, trying to decipher their meaning. They seemed to speak to her on a deeper level, a language beyond words.

Beneath the tree, nestled amongst the roots, Jessica found a small, moss-covered stone. It was smooth to the touch, and as she picked it up, she felt a surge of energy, a warmth that spread through her body. The stone was light, and as she held it, she felt a connection to the grove, the ancient trees, and the earth itself. It resembled a magical key, unlocking deeper global understanding.

Jessica sat beneath the giant tree for a long time, the stone resting in her palm. She closed her eyes, breathing, filling her lungs with the crisp, clean air of the grove. The sounds of the forest surrounded her—the rustling of leaves, the gurgling of the stream, the chirping of unseen birds—a symphony of nature's music. She felt a deep sense of peace and contentment, a profound connection to the natural world, a sensation that transcended the ordinary.

Jessica knew it was time to leave as the sun descended below the horizon, casting long shadows across the grove. In all its splendor, the grove had filled her with awe and wonder, a connection to something ancient and profound. She carried with her the memory of the humming energy, the vibrant colors, the gentle whispers of the trees, the secrets held within the ancient carvings, and the warmth of the magical stone.

The return trip felt shorter. The memory of the grove warmed her heart, the quiet energy of the place still resonating within her. She carried the stone, a treasure to remind her of the hidden magic within her backyard, a tangible link to the extraordinary world she had uncovered. As she emerged from the thicket of ferns, back into her familiar backyard, she realized that the world held countless hidden wonders, waiting to be uncovered by those who dared to look, listen, and believe in the surrounding magic.

She saw additional details she had not noticed before–the intricate patterns of the bark on the oak tree, the delicate veins in the leaves, the way the sunlight filtered through the branches. Each element of her backyard now possessed a unique charm, a story waiting to be uncovered. Her transformed landscape nestled the grove, which became her sanctuary. This sanctuary provided quiet contemplation and reminded her that even the most familiar places could hold extraordinary adventures. Jessica's journey had begun; her backyard and boundless imagination held a universe of possibilities, waiting to be explored.

Jessica talked about her discovery with her mother and grandmother the next day, describing the ancient grove. Her mother listened, her eyes wide with wonder, while her grandmother smiled, her expression hinting at a deeper understanding of the magical qualities of the natural world. They all agreed to explore the grove together, sharing this new wonder, strengthening their bond, and creating fresh memories together in this enchanted corner of their backyard. With her vast knowledge of plants and herbs, her grandmother helped Jessica identify some unfamiliar flowers and plants. They discussed the ancient symbols carved into the tree, exchanging theories and stories, their imaginations ignited by this newfound magical realm.

Jessica's neighbor, Señora Rodriguez, an immigrant from a country rich in folklore and nature-based traditions, shared stories of similar enchanted groves from her homeland, further enriching Jessica's understanding of the timeless connection between humans and nature. The grove became a shared warmth, weaving their stories into her world space, a testament to the power of imagination, intergenerational connection, and the rich tapestry of cultural understanding. The children from the neighborhood also joined their exploration, each adding their unique perspective and discovery to the ever-expanding world within Jessica's backyard. They created stories and legends about the grove, weaving their fantasies into the existing magic, filling the enchanted place with vibrant childhood dreams and adventures.

Exploration of the grove became a regular part of Jessica's life. Her activities included sketching the trees, identifying plants, and observing the wildlife. She learned to recognize the birdsong, the sounds of different insects, and the subtle changes in the light throughout the day. She developed a new appreciation for nature's quiet beauty, the interconnectedness of all living things, and the transformative power of observation.

The grove also inspired Jessica's creativity. She started writing stories about the ancient trees and their inhabitants, creating her mythology around the carved symbols and the magical stone. She drew detailed pictures of the flowers and plants, capturing their vibrant colors and intricate details. Her imagination soared, fueled by the rich tapestry of nature's wonders surrounding her.

Jessica learned to cherish nature's beauty, connect, and believe in its magic there. She also uncovered the most amazing adventures often hide in unexpected places, right in her own backyard. The magic of her backyard, and the secret garden within, continued to unfold, promising Jessica a lifetime of wonder, exploration, and endless possibilities, forever intertwined with the enchantment of the ancient grove.

Chapter 32: Encountering the Wise Old Owl

With each step Jessica took further into the dense grove, a growing feeling of excited expectation vibrated within her very being. Slender shafts of sunlight pierced the leaves, filtering through the branches and illuminating countless dust motes that swirled and danced in the air like miniature, glittering fairies. Trees towered, giant-like, over everything. Then she spotted the long-sought object.

Perched high in the branches of the largest tree, a magnificent owl sat regal and still. Its feathers were the color of twilight—a blend of deep grays, soft browns, and hints of silver, catching the light with an almost ethereal shimmer. Its eyes, large and luminous, seemed to pierce the shadows, holding an ancient wisdom that resonated deep within Jessica's soul. The owl was immense, its presence commanding yet calming, exuding an aura of serene power.

Jessica approached, her heart pounding a rhythm against her ribs. She had never seen an owl so large, so majestic. It sat still, a statue carved from moonlight and shadows, its gaze fixed on something beyond her. A long moment passed; she remained breathless, mesmerized by the creature's serene magnificence. Motionless, the owl silently guarded the grove's secrets like a sentinel.

Deliberately, the owl turned its head, fixing its gaze on Jessica. The eyes appeared to look beyond her surface, delving into her essence. Jessica felt a strange mixture of awe and nervousness. She was not afraid, but a deep respect filled her, a sensation of encountering something ancient and wise.

The owl hooted, a low, resonant sound that seemed to vibrate through the earth beneath Jessica's feet. The sound was not harsh or frightening; it was melodic, almost musical, carrying a sense of deep peace and understanding. It was a sound that resonated with the grove's ancient energy, a sound that spoke of centuries passed and countless seasons witnessed. The owl, soft yet deep-voiced, sounded like it called from the forest's core. declared, "You have reached the heart of Whispering Woods." Jessica gasped, taken aback. She had not expected the owl to speak.

"I... I did not expect you to talk," Jessica stammered, her voice a whisper.

The owl chuckled, a soft, rustling sound like dry leaves skittering across the forest floor. Many things are unexpected in Whispering Woods, child. This magical place holds secrets, blurring the boundaries between worlds.

Jessica felt a surge of excitement. She had encountered talking animals in her enchanted backyard, but this felt different. It felt deeper, older—a meeting with the grove's loyal protector. "How... how did you know my name?" Jessica asked, her curiosity overwhelming her surprise.

"Child, I know many things," the owl replied, its eyes twinkling with amusement from centuries of untold stories. "I have watched over this grove longer than you have been alive. Throughout my time, I have witnessed kingdoms rise and empires fall to dust. I have witnessed the passage of time itself."

The owl paused, turning its head, surveying the grove as if taking in its beauty once more. Children often came here seeking adventure, knowledge, and more.

"I... I am searching for something," Jessica admitted, "something beyond my everyday life. Something magical." The owl nodded. "Child, magic exists, but you don't always find it in grand gestures. Quiet moments, small details, and relationships reveal it."

The owl's cryptic puzzle that tested both heart and minds for Jessica grew difficult. The cryptic puzzle that tested both heart and minds was not simple word games; they were tests of Jessica's wisdom, her understanding of the natural world, and the knowledge she had gained on her journey through her enchanted backyard. The grove woven each cryptic puzzle that tested both heart and mind into its fabric, hiding its answer within the rustling leaves, the gurgling stream, and the ancient carvings on the majestic tree.

The opening cryptic puzzle that tested both heart and mind referenced the sun's path and its image in a stream. Jessica contemplated the puzzling enigma, its challenge both intellectual and emotional. She recalled sunlight shifting patterns within the grove. She studied the patterns of light and shadow, recognizing the answer reflected in the shimmering surface of the stream.

The second cryptic puzzle that tested both heart and mind spoke of the language of the trees, their silent communication, and their age-old wisdom. Jessica recalled her connection to the trees, the ancient carvings on the majestic tree's bark, the subtle energy she had felt pulsing through the grove. She understood the trees were speaking, not with words, but with their essence.

The third cryptic puzzle that tested both heart and mind involved the grove's creatures, their interdependence, and their roles in the ecosystem's delicate balance. Jessica recalled the tiny hummingbird, with its rapid movements and vital role in pollinating the flowers. She thought of the fish darting through the stream; the insects buzzing in the air, and the birdsong echoing through the trees. She understood the interconnectedness of life in the grove.

As Jessica solved each cryptic puzzle that tested both heart and mind, the owl nodded its approval, its enormous eyes gleaming with satisfaction. The owl shared its ancient wisdom with each correct answer, revealing more about the grove's history, secrets, and magical properties. Jessica uncovered the grove focused energy, blurring the boundary between realms; imagination soared, and dreams manifested.

The grove, the owl revealed, was not beautiful; it housed ancient knowledge, stories whispered across time. Ancient traditions, peaceful coexistence with the forest, knowledge through ages intertwined with nature's essence: the account detailed these. Sunset's long shadows draped the grove; the owl imparted wisdom: "Child, this place's magic requires nurturing, not discovery."

With a final, soft hoot, the owl spread its magnificent wings and disappeared into the twilight, leaving Jessica alone in the heart of Whispering Woods, carrying the wisdom and magic of the grove deep within her heart. The magical stone in her hand felt warmer, heavier, a tangible link to the magic she had encountered. The grove and the owl's words would forever remain etched in her memory, a reminder of the power of imagination, the wisdom of nature, and the endless possibilities that await those who dare to believe in magic.

Chapter 33: The Owl's Lessons and Guidance

The owl, its gaze unwavering, shifted, its massive head turning to show a path leading deeper into the grove. "The path ahead requires patience, child," it said, its voice a low rumble that seemed to vibrate through the leaves overhead. "You find true magic not through haste, but through careful observation," it said. She had always been a rather impatient child, preferring immediate gratification, but the owl's words resonated with a truth she felt.

The path the owl showed was visible, a narrow track winding between towering trees, their roots gnarled and ancient, reaching out like arthritic fingers. Jessica followed; her footsteps were soft on the moss-covered ground. The air grew cooler, damp, and the scent of wet earth and decaying leaves filled her nostrils. She paused, noticing minor details she had missed—a tiny mushroom sprouting from a fallen log, its cap a vibrant scarlet, a family of ants transporting crumbs along a hidden trail, the intricate patterns of lichen on the bark of the trees.

Sunlight filtering through the leaves created shifting patterns on the forest floor. She saw tiny wildflowers, their petals vibrant against the muted greens and browns of the forest. She listened to the forest's symphony, the rustling of leaves, the chirping of crickets, and the distant call of a bird. Sounds and sights offered profound, hidden meaning, revealed only to attentive observers. As she walked, Jessica imagined the owl's lessons were not about patience, observation, and understanding of the interconnectedness of everything within the grove. She saw the interconnectedness of everything within the grove. Intertwined tree roots, insects feeding flowers, birds feeding insects. It was a delicate balance, a complex ecosystem where every element was vital. She came across a small stream, crystal clear water flowing over smooth stones. Tiny fish darted through the shallows, their scales shimmering like jewels. Jessica kneeled beside the stream, cupping her hands to drink the refreshing water. As she drank, she reflected on the owl's words about protecting the natural world. She uncovered her magical backyard wasn't fantasy and adventure; it also presented a duty to nurture its inhabitants.

The path led Jessica to a clearing bathed in dappled sunlight. In the center of the clearing stood a magnificent oak tree, its branches reaching up towards the sky like arms outstretched in supplication. Beneath the oak tree, nestled amongst the roots, was a small carved wooden box. Jessica approached, her heart pounding with excitement.

She lifted the lid of the box. Inside, a bed of soft moss nestled a single, smooth, gray stone. It pulsed with a soft inner light. Jessica felt a lovely warmth blossoming in her hand. As she held it, she felt a surge of energy, a connection to the grove, the owl, and the magic surrounding her. The owl, following her, landed on a branch above. "This stone," it hooted, its voice comforted in the sunlight. "It holds a piece of the grove's heart. It will guide, protect, and remind you of the lessons you've learned."

The owl then guided Jessica through a series of challenges designed to test her understanding of the lessons she had learned—one trial with hidden stakes involved identifying different species of plants and animals based on their tracks and droppings. Jessica, remembering the owl's emphasis on careful observation, identified each one, her knowledge growing with every correct answer. Another trial with hidden stakes involved deciphering a series of symbols carved into the bark of an ancient tree. These symbols were not mere decorations; they represented a forgotten language — the language of the grove itself. The owl helped her understand the meaning behind the symbols, revealing a forgotten story — a legend about the grove's origins, its protective magic, and the importance of preserving its ancient secrets.

As Jessica progressed, she uncovered hidden pathways, secret waterfalls, and breathtaking vistas. The grove revealed its beauty to her in layers, revealing its secrets only to those who showed respect, patience, and a genuine love for nature. During her journey, Jessica also learned about the importance of community. She encountered other creatures in the grove—a wise old badger, a family of playful squirrels who tested her ingenuity with puzzles, and a solitary deer who showed her a hidden spring with the purest water she had ever tasted. Each meeting taught a lesson. Each connection reminded us of life's interconnection.

The owl continued to offer guidance, its words filled with ancient wisdom. It taught Jessica the importance of listening to the whispers of the wind, whispering secrets, understanding the language of the trees, and observing the subtle shifts in the grove's energy. The owl explained the grove was a living entity, filled with its unique magic and energy, which responded to the intentions and actions of those who entered. Treating the grove would reward them with its magic, but disrespect would cause its protection.

As the sun set, casting long shadows across the clearing, the owl landed before Jessica, its eyes gleaming with an ancient light. "Your journey through Whispering Woods has begun," it hooted, its voice soft but powerful. The grove harbors many secrets, many lessons. The owl's parting words, a proverb from generations of grove guardians, were: "Earth provides."

Chapter 34: A New Set of Riddles

The owl, perched on a branch above, its eyes gleaming like polished amber, hooted. "The path to the heart of the grove is not straight, young Jessica," it rumbled, its voice a low, resonant whisper. "It presents trials and cryptic puzzles that test your wisdom." Jessica, her heart pounding with excitement and a touch of apprehension, nodded. She was ready for a new trial with hidden stakes.

The initial enigmatic puzzle, challenged both emotions and intellect, resounded in the clearing, its message carried by the soft breeze among the rustling leaves: "I possess cities, yet no houses; What am I?"

Jessica pondered the cryptic puzzle that tested both heart and mind, the words swirling in her mind. Cities without houses... forests without trees... The answer came to her in a flash, a sudden illumination like a sunbeam piercing the forest canopy. "A map!" she exclaimed, her voice a whisper, filled with the thrill of discovery.

The owl hooted. "Indeed, a map," it confirmed. "A map is what you'll need to face your next trial with hidden stakes."

Jessica's eyes scanned the ground, examining each fallen leaf and mossy rock. Then she spotted it beneath the roots of a giant redwood, hidden by a curtain of ivy. A small, leather-bound map lay concealed, its edges softened by time and weather. Unfurling it, she examined the intricate details. It was not a map of any place she recognized.

Instead, it depicted a fantastical landscape, a whimsical world of twisting rivers, towering mountains, and luminous forests that seemed to pulsate with an inner light. The map itself was a cryptic puzzle that tested both heart and mind. As she traced its winding pathways with her finger, a new cryptic puzzle that tested both heart and mind emerged from the symbols etched into its surface, written in a language she did not understand, yet somehow knew. It was a series of symbols, each designed, representing elements from nature — sun, moon, stars, river, mountain, tree, and animal.

The message, but, was: The grove held the key: she must locate real-world equivalents to the map's symbols. The map's decoded symbols unveiled the second cryptic puzzle that tested both heart and mind: a visual puzzle, "Locate the sunrise's first touch, and the moon's evening secrets."

Jessica explored the grove, absorbing its subtle rhythms and harmonies. She followed the whispering streams, climbed sloped hills, her heart beating with anticipation and wonder. As twilight deepened, she uncovered a hidden clearing. A small pool of water still reflected the full moon. The surrounding trees seemed to glow with an ethereal light, creating a mystical, enchanted atmosphere. Solving the next cryptic puzzle depended on the pool; it tested both intellect and nerve.

She peered into the crystal-clear water. Its depths mirrored not moonlight, but a unique floral luminescence. This was her next clue. This image led her to the flower. She found it hidden amongst the lush vegetation—a flower that glowed with a faint, otherworldly luminescence, its petals veined with silver.

Next, a challenging puzzle, inscribed in glittering dewdrops on a luminous bloom, read: "I possess wings, yet flight eludes me." I have a voice but cannot speak. I whisper secrets to the wind, whispering secrets and dance with the sun. What am I?" This cryptic puzzle that tested both heart and mind was easier. The solution was straightforward: a seed. She acted on a hunch of the many seeds she had seen scattered throughout the grove, carried on the wind, whispering secrets, planted by birds, or left behind by passing animals. A seed was a symbol of new life, growth, and potential. The next clue would involve a seed.

Following the glimmering dewdrops left by the magic flower, Jessica uncovered a small, ancient oak tree, its bark furrowed with time. A single acorn, larger than any she had ever seen, nestled within its protective embrace, pulsating with a soft inner light. This acorn was unlike any other she had seen, radiating a quiet energy. Someone carved the fourth and final cryptic puzzle that tested both heart and mind into the shell of this magical acorn: "I am the beginning and the end, the silent observer, the keeper of secrets." This cryptic puzzle that tested both heart and mind was more abstract. She pondered nature's cycle: life, death, growth, decay—earth's quiet, sustaining presence.

She whispered her answer to the owl, who was observing her. "Time," she whispered, her voice steady. The owl nodded, its wise old eyes twinkling. "Indeed, child, time. And within the heart of time lies the ultimate treasure." The owl then guided her to a hidden cave behind the largest tree in the grove. A chest of carved wood was inside the cave, shimmering with crystals of all colors imaginable. A single, formed crystal ball was inside the chest, nestled on a bed of soft moss. It glowed with a warm, gentle light, pulsing.

As Jessica held it, a surge of energy rushed through her, a deep connection to the grove, its magic, and the earth itself. More than just a beautiful object, it was a conduit of the grove's wisdom and power. This was the true treasure.

Chapter 35: Solving the Owl's Riddles

The glowing acorn, nestled in the ancient oak's embrace, pulsed with a gentle light, a silent heartbeat in the grove's heart. Jessica traced the intricate carvings on its shell, feeling a strange warmth emanating from the smooth, hard surface. The final cryptic puzzle that tested both heart and mind, etched into the acorn's surface in delicate, shimmering lines, was profound, testing her intellect and understanding of the interconnectedness of all things. It spoke of beginnings and endings, silent observation, and secrets held close.

She sat beneath the oak; the sunlight dappling through the leaves, casting dancing shadows on the forest floor. She closed her eyes, breathing, letting the scent of damp earth and pine needles fill her lungs. Reflecting on her journey, she considered the challenges overcome and lessons learned. She recalled the map, a miniature world unto itself, its rivers mirroring the streams of the grove, its mountains echoing the sloping hills. She recalled the moonlit pool, where its surface acted as a mirror, reflecting the mysteries of the night. The luminous flower communicated its enigmatic secrets to the wind, whispering secrets, while the seeds dispersed by the breeze symbolized growth and potential.

The cryptic puzzle challenged intellect and spirit, its riddle: "I am present, yet invisible. What am I?" echoed in her mind. It was not a simple question with a simple answer. This enigmatic puzzle probed existence's core, focusing on life's cyclical journey. It demanded more than a quick solution; it required contemplation, reflection, and a deep understanding of the natural world.

Jessica reflected on the sun's daily trek through the sky, a steady symbol of passaging time marking the start and finish every day. The moon's phases, to her, symbolized cyclical change; a silent observer of unfolding seasons. The trees, their slow, steady growth, eventual decline, and return to the earth, their quiet presence, were a constant feature of the landscape she considered. She thought of the rocks, ancient and unchanging, yet bearing witness to eons of change.

Tiny seed packets, brimming with potential, held the promise of new life, a fresh cycle's start, in her thoughts.

The solution wasn't an object, instead, a comprehensive concept. Its influence formed the land, governed the seasons, and affected all life. It was the ever-present, yet unseen, presence that linked all things together.

A gentle breeze rustled through the leaves, whispering secrets only the forest could understand. Jessica opened her eyes, a quiet certainty settling within her. Truth unfolded, revealing itself. It was a revelation from her careful observation, thoughtful reflection, and growing connection to the natural world.

"Time," she whispered, her voice blending with the rustling leaves. Hanging in the air, the word offered a simple yet profound statement that captured the cryptic puzzle that tested both heart and mind's essence. It was the journey, not the puzzle's solution, that thrilled her.

High on a branch, the owl, its amber eyes gleaming, hooted in quiet approval of the dappled sunlight. Its silent acknowledgment was confirmation enough. It seemed to understand the depth of her answer, the understanding she had gained on her journey. It did not need words to express its agreement. The wisdom in its ancient eyes spoke volumes.

With a graceful sweep of its mighty wings, the owl descended from its perch, landing on a branch near Jessica. Its gaze held a warmth and benevolence she had recognized as the owl guided her. It seemed to share in her triumph, her successful completion of its intricate cryptic puzzle that tested both heart and minds. The owl's presence felt reassuring—a silent guardian, a wise mentor, a fellow traveler on this magical journey.

The owl then led her through a hidden pathway, concealed behind a curtain of ivy and ferns, a secret passage known only to those who possessed the wisdom to discover it. She followed, her heart filled with a mixture of anticipation and excitement. The owl's silent guidance instilled confidence, trust, and a sense of security.

They emerged into a clearing bathed in the soft, ethereal light of the late afternoon sun. Before her stood a massive redwood, its trunk wider than any she had ever seen, its branches reaching towards the sky like the arms of a benevolent giant. The tree exuded an ancient power, a timeless majesty. Even to her inexperienced eyes, it was clear this tree was ancient, a venerable patriarch of the grove, a silent observer of countless seasons.

The owl hooted again, showing a point behind the redwood's colossal trunk. Jessica moved closer, her eyes scanning the area for any sign of a hidden entrance, a secret passage. Then a barely visible crack appeared within the earth's mossy carpet. A hidden entrance, swallowed by the undergrowth, was visible.

Jessica went through the narrow opening, and the owl watched from a nearby branch. It led to a lit passage, the air cool and damp, fragrant with the aroma of the earth and stone. She felt a thrill of adventure as she stepped into the unknown. Twisting and turning, the passage sometimes narrowed to a crawl space, sometimes opened into small caverns, all bathed in a faint, ethereal glow emanating from the walls.

The soft, luminescent light emanating from the rock itself caused the passage walls to glow. The light was not harsh, but a gentle, calming radiance illuminated the path before her, guiding her deeper into the heart of the grove's hidden secrets. Crystals of every imaginable color—amethyst, quartz, ruby, emerald—sparkled like fallen stars, imbuing the passage with a mystical, otherworldly beauty.

A noticeable energy filled the air, a faint vibration coursing through her body. She could feel the ancient presence of the grove, its secrets whispered on the breeze, its wisdom echoing in the quiet depths of the cavern. This wasn't physical; it was spiritual, a descent into earthly energies.

The passage opened into an enormous cavern, its ceiling lost in the shadows, its walls shimmering with an incredible array of crystals. In the center of the cavern, bathed in the soft glow of the crystals, sat a chest made of carved wood, its surface gleaming with a deep, polished sheen. Its carvings looked ancient, depicting scenes of nature, animals, and mythical creatures.

The owl landed on the chest, its amber eyes twinkling in the dim light. Jessica approached, her heart pounding with anticipation. She reached out a trembling hand and lifted the heavy lid. Inside, nestled on a bed of soft moss, lay a single, formed crystal ball, radiating a warm, gentle light, pulsing with a rhythmic heartbeat.

It was a beautiful object and a conduit to the grove's energy, symbolizing its wisdom and power. Holding it, Jessica felt a surge of energy, a connection to the grove, its magic, and the earth itself. It was a tangible manifestation of her lessons—the importance of patience, observation, and the interconnectedness of all things. It was a reward not for her intelligence, but for her perseverance, her curiosity, and her unwavering belief in the power of her imagination. The crystal ball symbolized her journey, a testament to her growth, and a beacon illuminating her path to further adventures.

Chapter 36: Locating the Final Hidden Treasure

The crystal ball, warm in her hands, pulsed with a gentle rhythm, a silent heartbeat echoing the steady thump-thump-thump of her own excited heart. It felt like hers; a familiar feeling. The owl, perched on a nearby crystal formation, hooted, a sound that seemed to resonate with the humming energy of the cavern.

Jessica placed the crystal ball back in its mossy bed within the ornate wooden chest. She closed the lid, and the soft click was a final punctuation mark for this stage of her adventure. As if sensing her readiness to depart, the owl spread its magnificent wings and took flight, its silhouette a dark etching against the shimmering walls of the cavern. Jessica followed, retracing her steps through the glowing passage, the crystal's warmth lingering in her hand like a phantom touch.

Emerging from the hidden entrance, she found herself in the sun-dappled clearing, the redwood's massive form a silent sentinel guarding the grove's secrets. The owl had already ascended to its lofty perch, its watchful gaze seeming to follow her every move. It was time to share her discovery, to let others experience the wonder she had encountered.

As she walked back towards her world, the transformed backyard, she felt a shift in her perspective. The ordinary elements—the oak tree, the swing set, the flowerbeds—no longer seemed mundane. They held a more profound significance, echoing the magic she had encountered in the grove's heart. Her journey unearthed a deeper appreciation for the wonders hidden in the ordinary, a strengthened connection to nature, and a blossoming confidence in her abilities.

Reaching the edge of the "jungle," she found her grandmother sitting on the porch swing, a warm smile gracing her face. Her grandmother, a woman whose wisdom was as profound as the ancient redwood, seemed to understand the unspoken joy radiating from Jessica. She knew, without Jessica needing to explain, the transformative power of the journey undertaken.

"Tell me everything, my dear," her grandmother said, her voice gentle, her eyes sparkling with curiosity. Jessica, bubbling with excitement, recounted her adventure, describing the cavern's cryptic puzzle that tested both heart and minds, clues, hidden pathways, and breathtaking beauty. She described the owl, its silent guidance, and the connection she experienced in the earth's heart. She told her grandmother about the crystal ball, it's pulsing light, and the profound sense of peace and understanding it brought.

Her grandmother listened, offering a soft chuckle or a knowing nod. When Jessica finished her story, her grandmother smiled. "My dear," she said, "the greatest treasures are not always the ones you can hold. Sometimes, the most valuable treasures are the memories, the experiences, the lessons learned along the way."

Jessica's mother, who had been busy tending her flower garden, joined them on the porch. She, too, listened with rapt attention as Jessica retold her fantastical adventure. Her mother and grandmother embraced her, their love and support reinforcing the significance of her discovery. They did not question the fantastical elements of her tale; they celebrated her imagination and the strength she'd shown in facing challenges and solving the cryptic puzzle that tested both heart and minds.

The next day, Jessica talked about her adventure with her neighbors, the friendly immigrant families who lived nearby. She gathered them around the "magical river," the small stream running through her backyard. As she told them her story, each neighbor added their unique perspective, weaving their cultural tales and traditions into the narrative. They spoke of ancient myths, legends, hidden spirits, and mystical creatures.

A kind elderly woman, Mrs. Rodriguez, who had migrated from Mexico, shared stories of ancient Aztec legends, in which it was said that hidden treasures held the wisdom of generations. Mr. Patel, an Indian, discussed the sacredness of nature, the power of meditation, and the interconnectedness of life. They all seemed to understand Jessica's journey. Each offered their interpretation of the crystal ball's meaning, adding depth and richness to her understanding.

Days turned into weeks, and Jessica continued exploring her backyard world. Jessica transformed the swing set into her "pirate ship," the oak tree into her "towering mountain," and the flowerbeds into her "magical jungle." One afternoon, while exploring an undiscovered part of her "jungle," Jessica stumbled upon a hidden nook beneath a large rose bush. A small, carved wooden box lay tucked away in the soft earth. Resembling the cavern chest, yet miniature and wrought. Its lid was ajar, revealing its contents: small, smooth stones, each one radiating a different color and energy.

Jessica lifted the box, marveling at its craftsmanship. Each stone felt warm to the touch, pulsing with a gentle energy. The colors were vibrant and luminous, shifting as she held them. She recognized the stones as another form of the grove's magic, tangible reminders of the wisdom she had gained. Among the stones, she found a tiny, formed acorn, identical to the one that held the final cryptic puzzle that tested both heart and mind. This acorn held no cryptic puzzle that tested both heart and mind; instead, it contained a miniature crystal ball replica from inside the cavern. It was a perfect replica, gleaming with the same warm, gentle light, a miniature embodiment of the grove's energy. Holding the miniature crystal ball and collecting colorful stones, Jessica imagined that the veritable treasure wasn't the physical objects themselves, but the journey-the discoveries, the challenges, and the lessons learned.

Her backyard, transformed by her imagination, had become a gateway to a world of wonder, where the ordinary and the familiar became magical. And as she gazed upon her transformed backyard, the sun setting in a fiery blaze of glory, she knew her adventures were far from over. The magic continued, woven into the fabric of her everyday life, a testament to the boundless power of imagination and the enduring wonder of nature. The stories continued to develop, adapting to her experiences, growing with her, and always ready to bring fresh surprises. Each adventure brings a more profound understanding, a fresh discovery, and a new perspective on her surroundings. Her imagination, fueled by the natural world and inspired by the wisdom of her family and friends, would continue to carry her on countless more adventures, weaving magic into the everyday.

Chapter 37: The Significance of the Stones

The tiny, carved wooden box felt heavy in Jessica's hands. A gentle warmth radiated through her, a comforting embrace. She opened it; the lid creaked like an old door. Inside, nestled on a bed of soft moss, lay a collection of stones. They weren't ordinary stones, but vibrant and luminous, each a different color, shimmering with an inner light. There was a deep crimson stone, like a drop of ruby blood; a sapphire blue stone, as clear as a summer sky; a vibrant emerald green, echoing the lushness of the jungle; and a sunny yellow stone, warm and bright as a summer day. There were many more, each unique in color and subtle luminescence, holding its energy.

Jessica picked up the crimson stone first, as her fingers brushed its smooth surface. A warmth spread through her hand, a comforting sensation that seemed to flow into her heart. She closed her eyes, and a vivid image flashed through her mind–a field of poppies swaying in a summer breeze, their crimson petals catching the sunlight. She felt the sun's warmth on her skin, smelled the sweet fragrance of the flowers, and heard the gentle buzzing of bees. The intensity transported her to the field; she became a silent observer of its vibrant beauty.

Next, she picked up the sapphire blue stone. This time, the sensation was unfamiliar. An incredible calmness washed over her, a tranquil peacefulness that settled deep within her soul. She saw a vision of the ocean, the deep blue water stretching to the horizon, the waves lapping against the shore. She felt the cool spray on her face, smelled the salty air, and heard the soothing rhythm of the waves—profound serenity, oceanic vastness, and mystery, connected.

The emerald green gemstone augmented her energy levels, enhancing her overall vitality. She saw a lush forest teeming with life, sunlight dappling through the leaves, and birdsong filling the air in the trees. She felt the soft earth beneath her feet, smelled the damp scent of the forest floor, and heard the rustling of leaves in the breeze. A thrilling connection to nature's untamed beauty and outstanding power surged through them.

The yellow stone radiated warmth and happiness. A field of sunflowers stretched as far as the eye could see. Their faces turned towards the sun, their golden petals gleaming in the light. She felt the sun's warmth, smelled the earth, and heard leaves rustling. Joy, contentment, simple pleasures—that's what it felt like.

All stones had its own individuality, linked to various elements of nature. She realized that these weren't just pretty stones; they were conduits of energy, each one holding a piece of the grove's magic — a tangible connection to the power of nature. She felt a deep sense of wonder and gratitude as she had them in her hands, each pulsing with a gentle, life-giving energy. The stones felt like a collection of memories, each carrying the essence of a particular place, a specific moment in time, a unique experience. The crimson stone mirrored sun's warmth, ocean's calm, the forest's vitality, pure joy.

She repositioned the stones, creating a pleasing arrangement. As she did so, she felt a connection, a subtle energy flowing between them. The stones felt like a part of her now, an extension of her connection to nature, a reminder of the magic she had uncovered within her backyard. The tiny acorn, nestled amongst the stones, was identical to the one that had held the final cryptic puzzle that tested both heart and mind. But this one held no puzzle; it contained a miniature replica of the crystal ball she'd found in the cavern. It was a perfect copy, miniature yet glowing with the same warm, gentle light — a tiny beacon of magic, an echo of the energy she had felt deep within the earth. This miniature crystal ball felt like a key, not to unlock a door, but to unlock a deeper understanding of the magic she now held within her hands, within herself.

Holding the miniature crystal ball and the collection of stones, Jessica imagined that the veritable treasure wasn't the physical objects. It wasn't the gleaming crystal ball or the vibrant, magical rocks. Her ordinary backyard had become a magical gateway, a passageway into a world of wonder. Her imagination took flight there, transforming the ordinary into the extraordinary, imbuing the familiar with a sense of magic.

She looked out at her backyard, which her imagination had transformed into a fantastical landscape. Standing tall and proud, the oak tree was a majestic sentinel guarding her hidden grove. Swaying in the breeze was: The swing set, her pirate ship. Her vibrant jungle of flowerbeds buzzed with unseen creatures. Fiery orange and deep purple painted the sunset across the sky, casting long shadows on her transformed world. Blooming flowers and chirping crickets filled the air. It was a perfect ending to an ideal adventure.

As she gazed upon her enchanted backyard, she knew this was not the end of her adventures. The stones, the miniature crystal ball, and the memories of her journey would serve as reminders of the boundless power of imagination and the enduring wonder of nature. Her garden: a continuous source of inspiration, exploration, discovery, and creation. Her imagination, fueled by the natural world and the wisdom gained from her experiences, would continue to take her on countless more adventures, weaving magic into the fabric of her everyday life, one magical stone and one wondrous journey at a time. New opportunities, challenges, and stories would emerge each day. Magic had become an integral part of her, a loyal companion, a never-ending well of creativity, intertwined with the fabric of her existence. Unwavering certainty filled her; the best adventures were coming. The world held many undiscovered treasures; believing in magic unlocked them for those with vivid imaginations.

The stones seemed to pulse with a gentle energy, a subtle rhythm that mirrored her heart's beat. She felt a deep connection to them, a sense of kinship with the earth and all its creatures. Holding those stones, she felt strong, prepared. The journey had revealed physical treasures and unearthed a treasure within her — a newfound confidence, a deepened appreciation for nature, and a profound belief in the power of her imagination. The stones became more than pretty objects; they were tangible representations of the transformative power of her adventure, a constant reminder of the magic hidden within the ordinary. They were talismans, each holding a unique energy that resonated with the different facets of her being, a constant source of inspiration and strength. The magic continued to develop and grow with her, always ready to bring fresh surprises and wonders into her life.

Chapter 38: Understanding the Power of Nature

The miniature crystal ball, nestled beside the vibrant stones, pulsed with a soft, warm light. It differed from the larger crystal. As Jessica held it, a wave of understanding washed over her. The stones weren't pretty rocks but keys, each unlocking a different facet of nature's power. The crimson stone, for example, wasn't represent poppies; it held the sun's energy, the life-giving warmth that nurtured growth and brought forth vibrant colors. She could almost feel the sun's rays on her skin, the gentle warmth permeating her being. It was a sensation of pure energy, the essence of life itself.

The calm and calming sapphire stone connected her to the ocean's vastness, mysterious depths, and powerful currents. It wasn't the visual image of the sea she experienced; she felt the rhythmic pulse of the tides, the coolness of the water against her skin, the salty tang of the sea air. It was a sensation of immense power and profound peace, a reminder of the ocean's enduring strength. Holding it, she felt a sense of grounding, a connection to something ancient and vast.

The emerald green stone linked her to the forest's vibrant energy and vitality. She felt the damp earth beneath her feet, the rustling of leaves in the breeze, and the songs of birds echoing through the trees. It wasn't a visual image, but a sensory experience — a sensation of being immersed in the forest's vibrant ecosystem, a part of its intricate web of life.

The energy felt exhilarating, a powerful reminder of nature's resilience and ability to renew itself. The yellow stone, radiating pure warmth and happiness, connected her to the simple joy of a sunny day, the abundance of a field of sunflowers turning their faces towards the light. She felt the warmth of the sun on her face, the scent of blooming flowers filling the air, and the gentle buzzing of bees. Every day, miracles showcase life's beauty and simplicity, a sensation of pure contentment. I felt thankful for nature's gifts.

Jessica imagined she couldn't control or exploit the power of these stones. Instead, it was something to be respected, cherished, and understood. All stones held a unique energy, a different aspect of nature's power, and each deserved to be treated with reverence. She grasped true wealth wasn't ownership; These stones weren't mere objects; they linked her to nature's core, to the planet's rhythm.

This understanding deepened as she meditated with the stones, holding each one in her hand and sensing its unique energy. She closed her eyes, allowing the vibrations to flow, sensing their power and beauty. The more she connected, the more she realized how deeply intertwined her imagination was with the natural world. Her imagination wasn't separate from reality; it was a bridge, a gateway to understanding the hidden power and magic that surrounded her.

As the sun dipped below the horizon, painting the sky in vibrant hues of orange and purple, Jessica sat by her oak tree, now a majestic mountain in her imaginative world. She held the stones and the miniature crystal ball, sensing their gentle warmth. She realized that the veritable treasure wasn't about the rocks themselves; it was about the journey, the experience of discovery, the transformation she had undergone. Once an ordinary space, her backyard had become a magical realm of exploration and wonder.

The journey had taught her more than just the locations of hidden treasures; it had instilled in her the importance of respect, understanding, and a deep appreciation for the delicate balance of nature. She learned to connect with the world around her, listening to the whispers of the wind, whispering secrets, observing the patterns of the clouds, and sensing the earth's pulse beneath her feet. This experience fostered a profound appreciation for the interconnectedness of life. The stones she found became talismans—powerful reminders of her bond with the earth, rather than mere objects to be stored away in a box. She carried them with her on her walks, feeling their energies resonate with the trees, flowers, and creatures she encountered.

Excited to share her newfound understanding, she showed her grandmother and mother the stones and recounted her journey. They listened in fascination, marveling at her stories of talking butterflies, glowing crystals in a cave, and the magic she had uncovered in her backyard.

With their unique perspectives and stories, the immigrant neighbors added another layer of richness to her understanding of the world.

These stories deepened Jessica's appreciation for the diversity of cultures. She learned about different plants and animals, as well as unique traditions and beliefs, each offering a new perspective on the worldwide magic and wonder.

Jessica saw the power of nature reflected everywhere, not in her enchanted backyard. The way the sun warmed her face, the rain refreshed the earth, and the wind, whispering secrets rustled through the trees — each manifestation of nature's power — demonstrates its immense beauty and life-giving energy.

The miniature crystal ball, a constant companion, symbolized her inner strength and ability to transform her surroundings. It reminded her that the most potent magic came from within, from her imagination and ability to connect with the natural world. She understood that the veritable treasure was not the physical objects, but the journey of discovery, which transformed her perspective and deepened her connection to the Earth and all its creatures.

Jessica continued exploring her backyard, finding alternative paths, creatures, and aspects of nature's magic. She extended her explorations beyond her backyard, finding magic in the local park, the woods behind her house, and even the simple beauty of a single wildflower. The treasure she held wasn't a collection of stones and a miniature crystal ball; it was a boundless sense of wonder, a deep connection to the natural world, and an enduring belief in the power of her imagination. The magic lived on, growing with her, always ready to bring extra surprises and wonders into her life, forever woven into the tapestry of her experiences.

Chapter 39: Sharing the Treasure with Friends

The warm glow of the setting sun cast long shadows across Jessica's backyard, transforming her familiar landscape into a scene straight out of a fairytale. She clutched the four shimmering stones and the miniature crystal ball, their surfaces reflecting the fiery hues of the sky. She felt immense accomplishment, but a new thought blossomed in her heart—these weren't treasures to keep hidden.

The first person she thought of was Maya, her best friend. With her bright, curious eyes and boundless energy, Maya would appreciate the stones' magic. Jessica wrapped each stone in a soft piece of cloth, creating individual pouches that felt as special as the treasures within. She decided the crystal ball deserved its velvet-lined box.

The next morning, Jessica bounced to Maya's house, her excitement bubbling. Maya greeted her with a broad smile, her eyes sparkling with anticipation. Jessica unveiled the stones, explaining their connection to the sun, the ocean, the forest, and the simple joy of a sunny day. Maya gasped, her eyes widening in wonder as she held the crimson stone, sensing the warmth of the sun's energy radiating through her fingers. She felt the calm energy of the sapphire stone and the vibrant energy of the emerald stone.

She was as captivated by the stone's subtle hum as Jessica was. "It's like they're alive!" Maya whispered, her voice filled with awe. They spent the morning in Maya's Garden, each stone offering a unique view of the plants and flowers. The emerald stone, for instance, allowed them to hear the subtle whispers of the wind, whispering secrets rustling through the leaves, revealing secrets only nature could share. The sapphire stone helped them notice the intricate dance of bees and butterflies, each flitting from flower to flower with unseen purpose.

After her time with Maya, Jessica imagined the power of the stones extended beyond their energies. They were catalysts, sparking curiosity, igniting imagination, and fostering a sense of wonder.

Following that engagement, she had arranged a visit with her kind and senior neighbor, Mr. Rodriguez, a gentleman she held in high regard and who lived next door. He cultivated a small but vibrantly colorful herb garden, a delightful testament to his deep-seated love and appreciation for the natural world and all of its wonders. As Jessica approached him, her heart pounded in her chest, a mixture of excitement and a nervous apprehension filling her with a mix of emotions. Possessing gentle eyes and a warm smile, Mr. Rodriguez listened attentively, his expression shifting subtly from one of mild curiosity to one of deep and genuine interest. He meticulously examined each stone, his fingers carefully tracing the smooth surfaces with deliberate attention to detail.

Recalling his childhood in Costa Rica, he shared stories of lush rainforests, vibrant hummingbirds, and his people's deep connection with nature. He spoke of ancient traditions, explaining how his people revered the earth and its gifts, drawing knowledge and strength from its energy. The stones, he declared, were not pretty rocks; they were reminders of this ancient wisdom, a connection to something greater than themselves.

He held the yellow stone, his eyes closing in quiet contemplation. "This," he whispered, "reminds me of the warmth of the sun on my face, the joy of sharing stories with my family under the shade of a mango tree. It reminds us of the simple things in life, the treasures we often overlook." Sharing stories and the intertwining of cultures and experiences deepened Jessica's understanding and appreciation of the stones' significance.

Jessica also shared about her treasures with Mrs. Kim, who ran into the small bakery in the corner. The stones captivated Mrs. Kim, known for her warm heart and delicious pastries. She connected the sapphire stone's calmness to the rhythmic motion of kneading dough, the steady rhythm reflecting the ebb and flow of the ocean's tides. She connected the crimson stone to the fiery heat of the oven, its warmth transforming simple ingredients into culinary delights. Her insightful interpretations added another layer to the stones' magic.

It wasn't only her neighbors who benefited from this sharing. Jessica's grandmother loved the stones and their tales, captivated by Jessica's creativity.

She associated the emerald stone's energy with the tranquility she felt while sitting in her garden, surrounded by the smell of blooming jasmine and the songs of birds. Her insights, tinged with a lifetime of experience and wisdom, added another layer to Jessica's understanding.

Sharing the stones wasn't just an act of generosity. It was Jessica's way of building connections, forging bonds with her community, and deepening their shared appreciation for the natural world. Each person she welcomed into the experience brought their own story and perspective, enriching her understanding and expanding the collective knowledge of the stones' power.

The experience of sharing brought an additional dimension to Jessica's adventure. She saw the magic in the stones themselves and the connections they fostered. The rocks became bridges, connecting her to her friends, neighbors, and family, creating a powerful community centered on an appreciation of nature's incredible gifts. It offered a powerful reminder that the true treasure lies in connection, not possession. The stones became more than objects; they were symbols of unity, friendship, and the deep interconnectedness of life.

Jessica continued exploring new wonders in her backyard and beyond as the days turned into weeks. She continued sharing her experiences, knowledge, and the magic of the stones, her circle of friends and acquaintances expanding as her enthusiasm spread. Once a personal treasure, the rocks became a catalyst for wonder, and a testament to the power of imagination and the deep bond between humans and nature.

Jessica's adventures didn't end with the discovery of the stones. Instead, they developed, transforming into a series of interconnected experiences. Each stone became a seed of wonder, planting itself in the hearts of those who received it. The power of imagination and the simple sharing created an enduring legacy of wonder and connection. Jessica's story wasn't about the treasure itself, but the bonds it forged, and the enduring magic it ignited in the hearts of all who were lucky enough to share in it.

Chapter 40: The Treasure's True Value

The weeks that followed were a whirlwind of sharing and discovery. With her four shimmering stones and the miniature crystal ball, Jessica embarked on a mission to spread the magic she'd found. It wasn't about giving away pretty rocks; it was about sharing a connection to something larger than themselves.

Her next stop was the local library. The librarian, Ms. Evans, with her spectacles perched on her nose and a kind smile, listened as Jessica recounted her backyard adventure. A nature lover and a passionate literacy advocate, Ms. Evans saw the stones' potential. She suggested organizing a small workshop for children, a place where they could learn about the natural world and explore their creativity.

The workshop was a resounding success. Children, ranging in age from five to twelve, gathered around Jessica, their eyes wide with wonder as she explained the properties of each stone. They learned that the crimson stone represented the sun's energy; a reminder of warmth, growth, and the power of light. Evoking the tranquility of the ocean, the cool sapphire stone represented peace, patience, and the endless rhythm of the tides. The emerald stone symbolized the vibrant life of the forest, encouraging them to listen to the whispers of the wind, whispering secrets, observe the intricate details of nature, and appreciate the interconnectedness of all living things. The yellow stone, a symbol of simple joy, reminded them to find happiness in everyday moments — the minor wonders that often go unnoticed.

The success of the library workshop encouraged Jessica to expand her reach. She approached the local community center, proposing a series of nature walks led by her and her friends, each walk guided by the energy of one of the stones. The crimson stone walks, held during the sunniest parts of the day, focused on appreciating the warmth and power of sunlight. Participants learned about solar energy, the significance of photosynthesis, and the many ways sunlight sustains life. They learned about various types of plants, how to identify them, and the importance of respecting their delicate balance within the ecosystem.

The sapphire stone walks near the tranquil creek that runs through the park, promoting mindfulness and quiet contemplation. Participants learned about the significance of water conservation, the delicate balance of the aquatic ecosystem, and the calming influence of nature on the human mind. They also learned to appreciate the simple sounds of nature, the gentle murmur of the creek, the chirping of crickets, and the rustling of leaves.

The emerald stone walks took them into the heart of the forest, encouraging observation and a deeper appreciation for the natural world. Participants learned about the various trees, the animals that inhabit the forest, and the magnitude of biodiversity. The program encouraged participants to appreciate the subtleties of the natural world—wind whispers, insect dances, and the diversity of biodiversity.

Organizers filled the yellow stone walks with games and activities designed to promote joy and appreciation for the simple things in life. Participants played nature-themed games, created nature mandalas, and shared about their favorite moments in nature. These walks reminded everyone to pause, breathe, and appreciate the beauty surrounding them, fostering a sense of wonder and connection to the natural world.

News of Jessica's initiatives spread throughout the community. Her infectious enthusiasm and the positive impact of her actions captivated those around her. Local businesses offered their support, providing workshop materials and contributing to the community center's program funding. Jessica's initiative sparked a movement, a renewed appreciation for nature, and a vibrant sense of community.

One evening, while sitting with her grandmother on the porch, watching fireflies dance in the twilight, Jessica reflected on her journey. Once a personal treasure, the four stones had become catalysts for connection, fostering a deeper appreciation for nature and a powerful sense of community. The crystal ball, she realized, wasn't a magical artifact but a symbol of the infinite possibilities within each person's imagination. It reminded us that magic exists everywhere, in the everyday wonders of the natural world and in the shared warmth, weaving their stories into her world experiences that connect us to others.

Jessica's grandmother smiled, her eyes twinkling. "You've shown everyone, my dear, that the greatest treasure isn't something you find; it's something you create. It's the connections you make, the joy you share, and the wonder you inspire in others."

Jessica's adventures continued, each new experience building upon the last. She organized nature photography contests, led bird watching expeditions, and even started a community garden where people could cultivate their appreciation for nature. Her circle of friends expanded, her community strengthened, and the magic she'd uncovered in her backyard continued to spread.

The stones, however, remained special, not for their material value but for the memories they represented. They became symbols of the powerful bond between Jessica and her community, a testament to the incredible things that happen when we share our passion and inspire others to discover the world's wonders. The actual value of the treasure, Jessica felt, lay not in its possession but in the joy it brought to others, the connections it fostered, and the enduring legacy of wonder it left behind. It was a legacy that extended far beyond her backyard, reaching into the community's hearts and spreading a love for nature, imagination, and the boundless power of sharing. That, she realized, held immense, untold value, surpassing any gem.

The world, full of wonders, waited to be explored and shared, each story weaving into her own, one moment at a time. She understood now that the magic would ripple outward like water. Smiling, she knew this was the greatest adventure of all.

Chapter 41: A Backyard Celebration

The sun dipped below the horizon, painting the sky in orange, pink, and purple hues, as Jessica and her friends bustled about her backyard, transforming it into a fantastical celebration. The ordinary space, once the setting for her solitary adventures, was now abuzz with laughter, excitement, and the joy of a community.

Weeks of planning had culminated in this moment. Drawing upon the inspiration gained from her expeditions, Jessica envisioned a party unlike any other.

The oak tree, once a towering mountain in Jessica's imagination, was now adorned with shimmering fairy lights, transforming it into a magical centerpiece. Strings of colorful lanterns, reminiscent of the glowing crystals uncovered in the cave beneath the porch, hung from its branches, casting a warm, ethereal glow upon the scene. Jessica had arranged a collection of smooth, colorful stones around the base of the tree, each reflecting a memory, a lesson learned, or a moment of sharing warmly, weaving their stories into her world discovery.

Once a fearsome pirate ship sailing treacherous seas, the swing set now served as a whimsical refreshment station. Decorated with bright streamers and miniature pirate flags, it overflowed with homemade lemonade, sparkling juice, and an array of delectable treats. Next to it, a makeshift "treasure chest" overflowed with colorful cookies shaped like stars, seashells, and smiled suns—a sweet reminder of the treasures uncovered during their adventures.

Once a dense jungle teeming with imaginary creatures, the flowerbeds were now a vibrant display of nature's artistry. Jessica and her friends had arranged wildflowers and herbs, creating a colorful and fragrant tapestry that mirrored the beauty of the natural world. The scents of rosemary, lavender, and chamomile filled the air, adding a soothing and enchanting aroma to the festive atmosphere.

Seashells, collected during their sapphire stone walks, lined the pathways, creating a meandering shoreline that led guests to different activity stations. These stations encouraged interaction and creativity, reflecting the collaborative spirit that had blossomed within their community. One station featured a collaborative art project, where children could paint their interpretations of their favorite scenes from their adventures—a vibrant canvas of sharing warmly, weaving their stories into her world imaginations.

They dedicated another station to storytelling. Inspired by walks and explorations, the station encouraged children to share their own stories, fostering creativity and self-expression. Sitting under a canopy of twinkling fairy lights, Jessica's grandmother acted as the storyteller extraordinaire. She had prepared captivating tales about nature spirits, magical creatures, and the secrets hidden within the ordinary.

Ms. Evans, the librarian, set up a reading nook where children could browse nature-themed books and discover new worlds through the pages of their favorite authors. The books ranged from informative guides about the local flora and fauna to captivating tales about brave explorers and fantastical adventures. Ms. Evans, a skilled storyteller, wove her narratives with the enchanting elements of nature. They dedicated a separate corner to nature crafts. Under the guidance of a local artist, children created miniature terrariums, decorated painted pebbles with nature-inspired designs, and constructed bird feeders from recycled materials. Each creation reflected their unique creativity, connection to nature, and newfound appreciation for the environment.

As twilight deepened, Jessica's talented musician mother played her guitar. Her melodic tunes filled the air, creating a calming atmosphere that transitioned the celebration into a serene gathering under the star-lit sky. Night sounds melded with the music: crickets, owls, rustling leaves.

As the children danced under the stars like ancient watchers, their laughter blending with the music, Jessica's immigrant neighbors shared stories of their homelands, adding an international flair to the celebration. They spoke of their childhood's magical landscapes, unique traditions, and festivals.

The food was a delicious fusion of flavors, reflecting the cultural diversity of their community. Each dish represented a shared warmth, weaving their stories into her world experience, a connection forged through their common love for nature and storytelling. The aroma of spices and herbs wafted through the air, creating a symphony of sensations. A comforting and friendly ambiance enveloped the room.

As the evening drew to a close, Jessica stood amidst her friends and family, a sense of profound contentment filling her heart. The celebration had exceeded her wildest expectations. It wasn't a party; it was a testament to the power of imagination, celebrating community.

The four shimmering stones, placed on a small table, glowed in the moonlight, casting a radiant glow over the scene. They were not mere objects, but symbols of the transformative power of nature. They were a reminder that magic exists not in the fantastical realms of imagination but in the everyday moments of sharing warmly, weaving their stories into her world joy, connection, and communal spirit.

Jessica looked up at the star-filled sky, her heart brimming with gratitude. The night culminated in a bonfire, where stories and laughter danced in the flickering flames. Like miniature stars, the fireflies twinkled around them, casting their ethereal glow on smiling faces and the vibrant tapestry of their collective celebration. It was a night they would never forget, where their backyard transformed into a magical kingdom.

Chapter 42: Sharing Stories and Laughter

The air buzzed with the energy of sharing warmly, weaving their stories into her world experience as the bonfire crackled. Jessica, flushed with excitement, leaned forward, her eyes sparkling in the firelight. "My turn!" she announced, her voice brimming with enthusiasm. She launched into a tale of her encounter with the Whispering Willows, their leaves rustling secrets only she could understand. She described how the moonlight filtered through the leaves, transforming the familiar trees into ethereal sentinels guarding a hidden path to a sparkling stream. Her story, filled with vivid imagery and playful exaggeration, captivated her audience, each listener transported to the magical world she had created.

Next, Mateo, a boy with bright, inquisitive eyes, recounted a daring expedition to the "volcano"—a small mound of dirt Jessica had fashioned into a dramatic landscape. His story wasn't about mythical creatures or hidden treasures, but about the thrill of climbing to the summit and the breathtaking view he'd uncovered from the top. He spoke about the accomplishment and bravery that swelled within him as he conquered his fear of heights. His simple tale resonated, reminding everyone that adventure wasn't always about fantastical elements; sometimes, it was about overcoming personal challenges.

Anya, a girl with a quiet demeanor but a vibrant imagination, followed by a tale of a hidden glade she had uncovered amongst the flowerbeds. The wildflowers became tiny fairies in her story, their delicate petals shimmering with magical dust. She described secret conversations with butterflies, their painted wings whispering tales of distant lands. Her story was whimsical and magical, charming her listeners. Anya's contribution showed how even the quietest observers could transform the mundane into extraordinary tales.

The stories flowed, each as unique and captivating as the storyteller. Little Leo recounted his daring rescue of a lost ladybug, highlighting his newfound sense of responsibility and compassion. Sofia, a new friend, shared a story of her homeland, describing a vibrant festival filled with music, dance, and the aroma of exotic spices. Her story offered a global perspective, reminding everyone that they could find imagination and adventure anywhere in the world.

As the stories unfolded, the laughter intertwined with the crackling of the fire, creating a symphony of joy. Each narrative added a layer to the tapestry, highlighting the diversity of their imaginations and the universality of the human spirit. The children's tales weren't about fantastical creatures and far-off lands; they were about overcoming fears, forming friendships, and discovering the magic in everyday moments.

Ms. Evans, the librarian, captivated them with a story of a brave explorer who had uncovered a hidden waterfall in a remote rainforest. Her tale, filled with suspense, peril, and ultimate triumph, highlighted the significance of perseverance and courage. She emphasized the power of observation, the prominence of appreciating minor details, and the rewards of careful exploration, even in familiar surroundings.

Jessica's grandmother, a storyteller extraordinaire, wove a tale of mischievous sprites who lived in the old oak tree. Her story, filled with humor and playful mischief, reminded everyone that the fantastical could exist alongside and often enrich the ordinary. She highlighted nature's subtle sounds, revealing its secrets. Her story was a gentle reminder that even the oldest stories held new magic for those who listened.

Adults joined in, adding their own childhood stories to the mix. A whimsical story about imaginary friends, highlighting childhood imagination, was told by Jessica's mother. Jessica's dad highlighted the importance of teamwork and problem-solving. Neighbors joined in, sharing childhood memories, traditional games, folktales, and the beauty of their homelands.

These adult narratives enriched the tapestry, demonstrating how the power of imagination persists throughout life, not in childhood. They emphasized the prominence of storytelling in connecting across generations, bridging cultural divides, and strengthening community bonds. They served as a reminder that everyone possessed unique tales to share, each offering a fresh perspective on the world and its boundless possibilities. As the fire died, embers glowing like tiny stars, a sense of contentment settled over the group. That night showcased the community's strength.

The celebration's theme, that adventure and imagination are not limited to exotic experiences, highlighted locations, or fantastical creatures, emphasized a unique element of each story's overarching narrative woven into the evening. Mateo's tale of conquering his fear highlighted the substance of facing challenges and celebrating personal triumphs. Anya's whimsical story highlighted the power of seeing magic in everyday moments. Leo's ladybug rescue emphasized the importance of compassion and responsibility. Sofia's story offered a glimpse into different cultures and traditions. These diverse tales created a rich, multi-layered narrative that resonated with each participant, strengthening bonds and creating sense of community. The stories didn't entertain; they inspired. They ignited imaginations and encouraged creative thinking. Providing a platform for self-expression, they fostered confidence and a sense of belonging. The children learned from one another, developing their storytelling skills, expanding their worldviews, and fostering friendships that would last a lifetime. The adults reconnected with their childhoods and uncovered the ongoing power of imagination.

Jessica felt grateful as stars shone on the closing night. The celebration had exceeded her expectations. It wasn't just a party; it was a tribute to the strength of collective imagination.

Chapter 43: Celebrating Community and Friendship

The bright and clear morning dawned the next day. A gentle breeze stirred the oak leaves, remnants of last night's magic lingering. Jessica smiled, remembering the lively celebration. The unforgettable sensation of connection, captivating stories, and a sense of belonging. She found her grandmother in the garden, tending to her prize-winning roses. Jessica exclaimed, "Grandma, last night was perfect!" Her grandmother smiled, her eyes crinkling at the corners. "It was indeed a special night, dear one. The significance was not only in the stories but in the sharing. It was how you all came together, celebrating your imaginations and yourselves."

Jessica pondered this. She had felt a strong sense of community, a bond formed through laughter and mutual appreciation for each other's unique perspectives. The immigrant families from the neighborhood had brought a vibrancy to the evening, sharing stories of their homelands, traditions, and childhood memories. Señora Rodriguez recounted stories of mischievous river spirits from her childhood in Mexico, filled with wonder and cautionary tales. Mr. Chen, a quiet man with a twinkle in his eye, had shared a story of a legendary dragon protecting a hidden village in his native China. Each tale added a layer of richness and diversity to the celebration.

The stories displayed diversity. While Jessica had focused on the fantastical aspects of her backyard, Mateo's account of conquering the "volcano" had highlighted the courage found in personal challenges. Anya's story about the fairies in the flowerbeds highlighted the beauty in minor details. Little Leo's simple story had touched on essential themes of responsibility and compassion. Sofia, the new girl, had described the colors, sounds, and smells of her native Peruvian village, introducing them to a new culture through her enthusiastic storytelling.

Jessica imagined that this diversity was the true magic of the celebration. It was about sharing experiences and connecting with others, not about having the most imaginative story. Recognizing the distinctiveness of each person's viewpoint and input was crucial, celebrating the varied tapestry of their community. The adults' stories had added another layer of richness. Ms. Evans, the librarian, had woven a tale of adventure and perseverance, emphasizing the value of observation and exploration.

Jessica's parents, too, had shared stories from their own childhoods, illustrating how the power of imagination endures throughout life. Even their neighbors contributed personal stories, fostering a dialogue that spanned generations and cultures—the evening had been a powerful reminder that community wasn't about proximity but about connection. It was about finding common ground. Once a space, the backyard had transformed into a vibrant community hub where different cultures, ages, and personalities could gather and celebrate.

The celebration had also taught Jessica a valuable lesson about the significance of friendship. She had noticed how naturally the children had interacted with each other, sharing their tales and laughing together. There had been a genuine camaraderie and mutual respect for imagination and experiences. The friendships forged that night felt special, profound. It wasn't about playing together; it was about connecting on a deeper level, sharing their hopes, dreams, and fears. Sofia, the new girl, had found her place within the group, welcomed with open arms and genuine curiosity about her background. Her stories had opened their eyes to new cultures and perspectives, enriching their understanding of the world.

That morning, Jessica played with Sofia, sharing more stories about her backyard kingdom. They explored the "jungle" together, identifying fresh flowers and creating new narratives for the existing landscape. They found a giant ladybug, and Sofia, inspired by Leo's tale, placed it on a leaf. This compassion strengthened their bond.

Jessica imagined that the magic of her backyard hadn't faded with the sunrise. It had grown stronger, infused with the energy of sharing stories. The celebration showcased the power of imagination, building community, and fostering a sense of belonging.

Later that day, she visited Mateo, who lived a few doors down. They spent hours building a new structure near the "volcano, " this time a bridge spanning a "raging river"–a narrow ditch they camouflaged with twigs and leaves. They told an interesting story of trolls guarding the bridge, with voices like rustling leaves. Their collaborative storytelling added an extra dimension to their backyard adventures. They exchanged drawings and sketches of their fantastical creatures and imaginary lands, solidifying their new friendship.

Anya, with her quiet demeanor, joined them later. Together, the three friends crafted intricate fairy houses using acorns, twigs, and colorful pebbles. Anya's delicate touch and imaginative ideas transformed ordinary materials into enchanting dwellings, proving that the most magical things could come from simple things. Their quiet collaboration spoke volumes about their newfound friendship.

That evening, Jessica uncovered that her imaginative play wasn't a solitary endeavor, but a creative process that could blossom into strong friendships and a more profound sense of community. Collaborative storytelling, laughter, and mutual appreciation were the veritable treasures of her backyard kingdom. The experience mattered less for its fantastical elements than for the companions she enjoyed them with.

As the sun dipped below the horizon, casting long shadows across her backyard, Jessica sat on the swing set, now a pirate ship, only in her imagination. She thought about the laughter they had enjoyed, and their connections. Sharing tales, forging connections, and blending imagination with friendship showed the world's potential. She was sure that this signified many enchanting evenings, weaving their stories into her world escapades, and countless tales in the ordinary yet extraordinary setting of her backyard. The ongoing adventure would be the ever-developing tapestry of friendship and community.

Chapter 44: The Power of Belief

The following days were a whirlwind of imaginative play. Emboldened by the success of her backyard celebration, Jessica transformed her surroundings. A simple pile of leaves became a dragon's hoard, its glittering treasures shimmering in the afternoon sun–sparkling dewdrops, but to Jessica, they were priceless jewels. The old garden gnome, overlooked, became the wise king of a hidden kingdom, dispensing a cryptic puzzle that tested both heart and minds and offering cryptic advice (squeaks and wobbles).

One afternoon, while exploring her "mountain"–the oak tree–she uncovered a tiny bird's nest tucked among its branches. She examined it, her imagination transforming the delicate construction into a breathtaking castle built by small, winged architects. The fragile twigs and leaves became intricate towers and ramparts, defended by fierce, though miniature, dragon-like guards (again, imaginary). This act of observation, this careful appreciation of the natural world, further fueled her creativity.

She noticed details she had never seen before. The intricate veins on a leaf, the delicate patterns on a butterfly's wing, the way the sunlight filtered through the leaves, creating dancing shadows on the ground. Each observation ignited a new story, a new adventure. A fallen log became the hull of a pirate ship; its splintered wood, rough-hewn planks, were perfect for a thrilling voyage across the "raging river" (still camouflaged as a ditch). She drew, filling notebooks with sketches of her fantastical creatures, her imaginary landscapes, her ever-growing kingdom.

Mateo, ever practical, helped her build elaborate fortifications around her castle using twigs, stones, and sculpted mud bricks. Anya added delicate details to the landscape through her quiet observation, creating miniature gardens with fantastical flowers crafted from petals and small pebbles. Inspired by the vibrant colors of her Peruvian homeland, Sofia painted whimsical murals on the castle walls, adding splashes of exotic brilliance to the already fantastical setting.

Their collaborative storytelling flourished. They no longer told stories; they lived them. As explorers, they charted unknown territories; as pirates, they plundered treasure; and as knights, they defended their kingdoms. The boundaries between reality and imagination blurred.

One evening, as the sun set, casting long shadows across the backyard, Jessica recounted her thrilling escape from a giant spider (a huge garden spider, in reality), her daring rescue of a damsel in distress (a lost ladybug, returned to a safe leaf), and her eventual triumph over the evil sorcerer (a grumpy garden snail).

Her mother listened, her eyes twinkling with amusement and admiration. "You know, Jessica," she said, "your imagination is powerful. It allows you to create entire worlds, to solve problems, and to experience things beyond your everyday life. But it's not about escaping reality; it's also about understanding it better."

Jessica pondered this. She realized that her imagination wasn't a way of avoiding the real world, but a means of engaging more deeply with it. Her adventures in the backyard taught her to observe the natural world, appreciate its beauty, and understand its complexities. She'd learned about different types of flowers, the habits of insects, and weather patterns. Her imaginary kingdom had become a lens through which she saw and understood the world around her.

"It's about believing in yourself, too," her mother continued. "You can create, imagine, and achieve anything you want. Don't let anyone tell you otherwise." These words resonated with Jessica. She realized that the confidence she gained from her imaginative play translated into other aspects of her life. She felt more self-assured, more capable, more willing to take risks.

This newfound confidence extended beyond her backyard. At school, she was more willing to take part in class discussions, share her ideas, and overcome her shyness. She found her voice, not in her imaginative narratives, but in her everyday interactions. She uncovered that the same creativity that fueled her fantastical adventures could also help her solve everyday problems–from working on a complex math problem (with the help of some imaginary helpful fairies, of course) to figuring out how to manage a conflict with a classmate (with the help of her imaginary council of wise gnomes).

After noticing the change in her granddaughter, Jessica's grandmother encouraged her even more. She emphasized the importance of self-belief and imagination in overcoming challenges and achieving ambitions. She reminded Jessica that the most extraordinary adventures often begin with a simple act of imagination—a seed of belief planted in the fertile ground of the mind.

Jessica felt her grandmother's words. She realized that imagination wasn't a childish fantasy, but a powerful tool, a source of strength, creativity, and resilience. It fostered self-connection, global awareness, community, friendship, and meaningful moments. It was a pathway to self-discovery and self-belief.

One day, while sketching her fantastical creatures, she created a special book. It would be a collection of her stories, drawings, and adventures. She called it "The Chronicles of the Backyard Kingdom." It became a tangible expression of her imagination, a testament to the power of self-belief and the extraordinary adventures that await those who dare to dream.

Every page showcased her world, highlighting the transformative power of creativity, community, and imagination. Her story ignited similar sparks in others; Mateo started writing adventure stories, Anya drew fantastical landscapes, and Sofia created intricate paper sculptures inspired by the creatures of Jessica's kingdom.

The power of imagination can transform ordinary experiences into extraordinary memories, fostering a sense of community and deepening friendships. Jessica learned that the power of self-belief wasn't about believing in one's abilities; it was about believing in oneself. The backyard, once a space, had become a place where the ordinary became extraordinary, fueled by the power of belief and the boundless capacity of the human imagination. And it was a journey that continued, unfolding day by day, adventure by adventure, story by story, within the hearts and minds of friends.

Chapter 45: A Lesson in Self-Discovery

Jessica's ever-growing backyard kingdom filled the summer days with vibrant hues. Her initial explorations had blossomed into a deeper understanding of herself and the world around her. She wasn't playing; she was learning. Each imaginary encounter, each solved a cryptic puzzle that tested both heart and mind, each fantastical creature she conjured revealed a new facet of her personality.

One sweltering afternoon, while attempting to scale her "volcano" (a rather large anthill), Jessica stumbled upon a colony of ants carrying crumbs back to their nest. She had planned to incorporate the anthill into her pirate adventure, perhaps as a hidden treasure cave. However, watching the ants, their tiny legs moving with relentless purpose, sparked a different narrative in her mind.

Imagining herself as an ant, she navigated the vast, towering grass blades that formed a jungle in her miniature world. She magnified the challenges they faced—crossing streams (miniature puddles), climbing mountains (fallen twigs), avoiding predators (larger insects)—into epic struggles in her imagination. She understood their tireless work ethic, unwavering collaboration, and deep connection to their community. This became serious.

This newfound empathy extended beyond the ants. While observing her backyard, she noticed the struggles of other creatures: a lonely ladybug searching for a leaf, a caterpillar inching across the ground, and a bird struggling to feed its young. She imagined their perspectives, challenges, and triumphs. She rescued the ladybug by placing it on a safe leaf and provided a small sanctuary for the caterpillar from the looming shadow of a hungry bird.

These minor acts of kindness were not acts of play; they were gestures of genuine compassion, born from her heightened awareness and growing empathy. She realized that her imagination was a tool for creating fantastical worlds and a window into the lives of others, both real and imagined.

Her interactions with her friends also deepened. As always, the meticulous planner Mateo began incorporating his newfound empathy into their games. He constructed insect shelters, created miniature waterways for the ants, and designed elaborate rescue missions for distressed creatures. Anya created detailed illustrations of the insects with her artist's eye, capturing their intricate features and unique personalities. Sofia, inspired by her grandmother's stories of the Peruvian Andes, wove tales of magical creatures and hidden valleys, enriching their adventures with a vibrant tapestry of mythology and folklore.

Their collaborative storytelling became even more profound. They weren't creating stories; they were co-creating a world filled with kindness, collaboration, and mutual respect. Their adventures weren't about conquering challenges; they were about understanding the challenges faced by others, both in the imaginary world they created and the real world around them.

One evening, as they shared stories about their latest adventure—a daring rescue mission to save a stranded butterfly from a spider's web — Jessica's grandmother joined them. She listened as they recounted their tale, her eyes sparkling with appreciation. She praised their teamwork, creativity, and compassion. "You know, children," she said, her voice gentle but firm, "the greatest adventures aren't always about conquering dragons or finding buried treasure. Sometimes, the greatest adventures are discovering the hidden treasures within ourselves and the world."

Her words resonated with Jessica. She realized her journey wasn't about conquering imaginary foes or building fantastical kingdoms. It was about learning, growing, and discovering the power of empathy, the strength of collaboration, and the beauty of sharing warmly, weaving their stories into her world experiences.

That night, Jessica lay in bed, her mind buzzing with thoughts. She had uncovered an extra dimension to her imaginative play. It wasn't about escaping reality, but about enriching, understanding, and connecting with it on a deeper level. Her imagination sharpened her worldview, fostering clarity, compassion, and understanding. She filled the following days with a renewed sense of purpose. Jessica found deeper meaning; empathy and responsibility shaped her journey. She saw her backyard not as a playground, but as a vibrant ecosystem teeming with life, a complex web of interconnected beings.

Her creativity flourished. A more profound sense of understanding and appreciation for the natural world imbued her with new characters, scenarios, and adventures. Starting with the author's actions: Her stories detailed the ants' struggles and triumphs, the butterflies' journeys, and the wisdom of the old oak tree. She drew detailed sketches of the insects, capturing their unique features and personalities. She even started a small garden, tending to the plants, creating a haven for the creatures of her backyard kingdom.

Her self-discovery was not just an internal journey, but also a journey of connection. She inspired others to see the world in new and meaningful ways. She learned that her imagination wasn't a personal escape but a powerful tool for connecting with others, building bridges, and fostering a community.

Sharing her gifts, creativity, and empathy with others became a vital part of her life. It was no longer about her journey of self-discovery, but a shared warmth, weaving their stories into her world journey of collective understanding and mutual support. Her imagination had become a conduit for connecting with others, fostering empathy, and celebrating the world's richness and diversity.

Her book, "The Chronicles of the Backyard Kingdom," continued to develop, reflecting her adventures, and their collaborative storytelling efforts. Each chapter was a testament to their journey of self-discovery, celebrating their unique gifts and talents, a tribute to the power of the transformative strength of empathy.

Once a simple space, the backyard had become a rich tapestry of experiences, a vibrant ecosystem of imagination and empathy, a place where the ordinary became extraordinary, and where the power of belief transformed simple play into profound self-discovery. The adventures continued, unfolding day by day, story by story, deepening her understanding of herself and the world, strengthening her bonds with her friends and family, and solidifying her belief in the transformative power of her imagination.

Chapter 46: Reflecting on the Journey

The late afternoon sun cast long shadows across Jessica's backyard, painting the familiar landscape in hues of orange and gold. She sat on the worn wooden steps of her porch, the "Cave of Glowing Crystals" (a spacious space under the porch) behind her, a silent witness to her incredible summer. A gentle breeze rustled the leaves of the "Whispering Willows"- a row of expressive weeping willows - their branches swaying as if whispering secrets to the setting sun.

It had all been so extraordinary. Transforming her ordinary backyard into a fantastical kingdom, teeming with imaginary creatures and hidden treasures, now felt almost surreal, like a dream from which she was awakening. Yet, the Evidence was all around her: the crafted miniature shelters Mateo had built for the insects, Anya's vibrant drawings depicting the personalities of her insect friends, and they tended the garden where she nurtured her little corner of the backyard ecosystem. These were tangible reminders of a summer filled with wonder, discovery, and the unwavering power of her imagination.

She thought back to the first day, her hesitant steps into her self-created world, the nervous anticipation as she navigated the "Towering Mountain" (the oak tree), the trepidation she felt as she sailed her "Pirate Ship" (the swing set) across the "Ocean" (the lawn). Those early adventures showed a childlike sense of wonder and a playful exploration of her creativity. But the journey hadn't been about play; it had been a profound journey of self-discovery.

She had learned so much about herself this summer. She'd uncovered her resilience, capacity for empathy, and the surprising depth of her imagination. Scaling the anthill, intended as a simple pirate adventure, had instead transformed into a journey of perspective-taking, allowing her to understand the ants' tireless work ethic and collaborative spirit. She'd witnessed the silent struggles of other creatures–the ladybug, the caterpillar, the birds–and found herself moved by their vulnerability. Her compassion blossomed, fueled by her heightened awareness and ability to step into their worlds through her imagination.

Her forged friendships were as invaluable as the treasures she had found. With his meticulous planning and endless enthusiasm, Mateo had brought a strategic depth to their adventures. Anya's artistic eye had breathed life into the fantastical creatures they created, bringing them into existence with her vibrant drawings. With her rich storytelling ability, Sofia had woven tales of Peruvian mythology into their adventures, adding depth and cultural richness to her world.

Their collaboration had been more than playful interactions. Learning to listen, value one another's perspectives, and work together toward common goals, they had become a cohesive unit. They hadn't conquered imaginary challenges; they had learned to navigate them with kindness, empathy, and mutual respect.

Her grandmother's words still resonated within her: "The greatest adventures aren't always about conquering dragons or finding buried treasure. Sometimes, the greatest adventures are discovering the hidden treasures within ourselves and the world." Those words were a turning point, showing her that the genuine treasure wasn't gold, but her personal growth, friendships, and understanding.

The impact extended beyond her immediate circle. Her neighbors, Mrs. Rodriguez and Mr. Kim had enriched her understanding of different cultures, expanding her worldview and fostering a sense of connection with people from various backgrounds. Sharing her stories with them had been as rewarding as the adventures themselves. They had listened with rapt attention, offering encouragement and sharing their childhood memories, weaving their narratives into the rich tapestry of her backyard kingdom.

She looked up at the sky, the first stars beginning to appear, twinkling like the glowing crystals in her imagined cave. The summer's adventures hadn't been about imaginative play; they had been a powerful metaphor for life. She had faced challenges, overcome obstacles, built friendships, and learned valuable lessons about herself and the world around her. These lessons extended beyond the realm of fantasy.

"Backyard Kingdom" developed, transitioning from fictional adventures to a personal growth record that showcases the impact of imagination and the worth of friendship. Each chapter, conceived as a separate adventure, now flowed together, forming a cohesive narrative of self-discovery and their stories into her world experience. The act of writing itself had been an invaluable part of the process.

It had allowed her to reflect on her experiences, analyze her emotions, and articulate the profound lessons she had learned. The words flowed now, guided by her memories and enriched by the perspectives of her friends and neighbors.

As darkness deepened, she went inside, the image of her backyard kingdom etched in her mind. She understood further adventures awaited. Once a simple space, the backyard would continue to be a canvas for her imagination, a space where ordinary objects could transform into extraordinary places, a stage for endless adventures. The stories, too, would continue. Her journey of self-discovery, fueled by the boundless power of her imagination, was only beginning. With a warm certainty in her heart, she knew that many adventures and stories awaited discovery, writing, and sharing. The real and imagined worlds were vast, brimming with untold possibilities, and she was ready to explore.

Chapter 47: A Renewed Sense of Wonder

Redolent of wood smoke and baked bread, the comforting aroma drifted from Mrs. Rodriguez's house, mingling with the cool night air. Jessica, tucked into her bed, felt a profound sense of contentment. The summer had ended, school had begun, but the echoes of her backyard adventures still resonated within her. It wasn't the fading sunlight on the "Towering Mountain" or the rustling whispers of the "Willows" that lingered; it was the profound shift in her perspective.

Her backyard wasn't a backyard anymore. It was a limitless expanse, a world waiting to be explored, reimagined, and rediscovered with each passing season. That mighty oak resembled a castle, spaceship, or hidden temple. She could transform her trusty pirate ship swing set into a flying machine, a magical carousel, or a queen's throne. The flowerbeds, her jungle, could bloom anew with fantastical flora, each petal holding a secret, each leaf whispering tales of ancient times.

This renewed sense of wonder wasn't about the physical transformation of her backyard. It was a deeper understanding of the power of her imagination, its limitless capacity to reshape the ordinary into the extraordinary. She realized that her ability to transform her surroundings wasn't child's play; it was a skill, a creative muscle she could strengthen and develop. The adventures hadn't ended with the summer; they had begun.

The possibilities were overwhelming, thrilling, and daunting. Exploring the "Cave of Glowing Crystals," she could discover new passages, unearth new treasures, or even encounter fascinating creatures. She could sail her "Pirate Ship" across uncharted waters, battling imaginary sea monsters, discovering lost islands teeming with exotic plants and animals. She could climb the "Towering Mountain" and find new peaks, hidden valleys, and breathtaking vistas, each revealing a new chapter in her ongoing saga.

"The Chronicles of the Backyard Kingdom" started a larger story. Envisioned as a record of her summer adventures, the journal became a testament to the boundless potential of her imagination. She had learned to weave words like magic, conjuring vivid images and emotions that transported the reader into her fantastical world. Every character receives a meticulous description;

And it wasn't the written word that captured her imagination.

She started sketching her backyard, each drawing capturing the essence of its potential. One drawing depicted the oak tree as a majestic castle, its branches reaching up to a starry sky. Another showed the swing set soaring through the air, transforming into a fantastical flying machine. A third drawing captured the flowerbeds at night, illuminated by glowing mushrooms and mythic creatures. The sketchbook became her map of infinite possibilities, a tangible expression of her boundless imagination.

She added more elements to her backyard world. Miniature bridges spanned the garden hose, which she imagined as a "river," and she built tiny houses for her imaginary friends. She decorated the "Cave of Glowing Crystals," transforming it into a magnificent underground palace. These additions weren't physical enhancements but tangible manifestations of her imagination, making her world even more real and captivating.

Her friendships had deepened, too. Mateo, Anya, and Sofia joined her in these recent adventures. Mateo's strategic mind began devising elaborate plans for their imaginary journeys. Anya's artistic talents blossomed, creating vibrant maps and illustrations. Sofia's storytelling skills introduced new legends and myths from diverse cultures, enriching their adventures with rich perspectives and nuanced cultural insights.

One afternoon, inspired by a book on ancient civilizations, they transformed their backyard into an ancient Egyptian city. They used cardboard boxes to create pyramids, arranged pebbles to form hieroglyphs, and draped fabric over the bushes to create the illusion of ancient temples. Mateo, acting as the architect, planned the city layout, ensuring that each building had a purpose and a historical context. As an artist, Anya decorated the pyramids with colorful symbols and hieroglyphs, bringing the city to life with her vivid artistic interpretations. Sofia, acting as the historian, shared tales of pharaohs, gods, and goddesses, adding a mystical depth to their adventure.

Their collaboration was seamless. It wasn't just about playing games anymore. They were creating something amazing, side by side. Jessica, empowered by her newfound confidence, took the lead, guiding her friends through the intricacies of their self-created Egyptian world.

The ordinary became extraordinary, and the familiar transformed into a breathtaking exploration of history and myth. The impact of their adventures extended beyond their backyard. They invited their neighbors to contribute their own stories. Ms. Rodriguez shared memories of her childhood in Peru, weaving Andean mythology into the fabric of their Egyptian-themed city. Mr. Kim, a talented woodworker, brought his craftsmanship to life by creating miniature replicas of ancient Egyptian artifacts. These interactions enriched their understanding of diverse cultures and traditions, fostering a global perspective on the power of imagination and the importance of collaboration.

Jessica learned that her imagination wasn't a personal tool for escape and self-expression, but a powerful force for connection and community building. Sharing her creative world with others allowed her to connect with them on a deeper level, bridging cultural differences, and fostering friendships.

As fall leaves fell, painting the backyard in vibrant hues of red, orange, and gold, Jessica knew her adventures were far from over. The changing seasons brought new possibilities, challenges, and opportunities to explore the boundless world of her imagination. The backyard, once a simple space, had become an infinite canvas. Here, ordinary objects become extraordinary adventures. At this stage, endless possibilities for imaginative exploration and personal growth lie ahead. The stories would continue, the friendships would endure, and the journey of self-discovery, fueled by her boundless imagination, would continue its exciting course. The real and imagined worlds were vast, brimming with untold possibilities, and Jessica, armed with her imagination and the support of her friends, was ready to embark on an exploration. Wonder, for her, became a constant, not a fleeting summer emotion.

Chapter 48: The Enduring Power of Imagination

The crisp fall air nipped at Jessica's cheeks as she stood at the edge of her backyard, a sketchbook clutched in her hand. The vibrant summer hues had faded, replaced by a palette of warm browns, fiery reds, and golden yellows. Once green, the leaves crackled underfoot, a symphony of rustling whispers announcing the changing season. Yet, the magic hadn't faded. It had transformed, shifting and adapting to the rhythm of nature itself.

Her backyard, once a sun-drenched kingdom of summer adventures, now held the promise of a different enchantment. Now adorned with a crown of russet leaves, the towering oak seemed to beckon her towards new mysteries. The whispering willows, their branches bare against the twilight sky, seemed to hold secrets whispered on the wind, whispering secrets. The flowerbeds, once vibrant jungles, were now a tapestry of muted colors, their dormant seeds promising a burst of new life in the spring.

But Jessica saw more than the physical changes. She saw potential, a canvas waiting for her imagination to paint upon it. The mist and mystery enveloped the oak tree like a haunted castle. Spectral guardians, the willows could become, their branches reaching like skeletal fingers. The flowerbeds, transformed, would become a mystical graveyard, home to whispering spirits and glowing fungi.

This understanding, this deep-seated knowledge of her imagination's power, wasn't a childish fancy. It was a revelation, a key that unlocked a world of limitless possibilities. She realized her imagination extended beyond her backyard. A simple walk to school could become a perilous journey through a dark forest filled with mischievous sprites and talking animals. She could transform her classroom into a magical academy, where students cast spells and brewed potions. Even the mundane tasks of homework and chores could become quests, challenges to overcome with courage and wit.

This newfound understanding sparked a creative fire within her. Her backyard adventures incorporated elements from the changing season. Using fallen leaves, she created intricate mosaics on the ground, depicting fantastical creatures and mythical scenes. She collected colorful acorns and pebbles, transforming them into miniature treasures and magical artifacts. She even fashioned tiny scarecrows out of twigs and leaves, each guarding a hidden secret or a whispered clue.

This enduring magic captivated her friends, Mateo, Anya, and Sofia. Employing his strategic mind, Mateo started designing elaborate obstacle courses through the autumnal landscape, using fallen branches, rocks, and leaves as elements of the trial with hidden stakes. With her artistic flair, Anya began painting vibrant murals on the shed's walls, depicting scenes from their autumnal adventures—brave knights battling fearsome dragons, mischievous fairies dancing under the moonlight, and wise owls dispensing cryptic clues. With her storytelling prowess, Sofia began weaving tales of fall spirits and mythical creatures that inhabited their backyard.

Their collaborative efforts transformed their backyard into a living testament to their boundless imaginations. One afternoon, inspired by a book on folklore, they created a haunted forest in their backyard. They constructed spooky pathways using fallen branches, creating a maze that twisted and turned through the trees. Anya painted eerie faces on pumpkins, placing them along the paths, their glowing eyes seeming to watch their every move. Mateo devised a series of a cryptic puzzle that tested both heart and minds and puzzles, hidden among the leaves and branches, that led to a collection of fall-themed trinkets they had gathered. As the narrator, Sofia spun tales of ghostly apparitions and mischievous spirits, filling the air with whispers of the supernatural.

Their collaborative spirit extended beyond their immediate neighbors. Jessica, empowered by her confidence and inspired by the rich diversity of stories around her, started documenting their adventures in "The Chronicles of the Backyard Kingdom" and added a new chapter to the ongoing story. This wasn't a record of their playful escapades, but a testament to the power of imagination as a bridging force between cultures — a tool for fostering understanding and empathy. Each entry in her journal showcased a new adventure, a different transformation of their backyard, and a new perspective gained. It was a testament to the richness and depth of their collective imagination, reflecting how their unique perspectives enriched the stories they created together. It chronicled their collaborative storytelling, weaving diverse cultural elements and the playful merging of fantasy and reality. Jessica's writing strengthened, becoming more nuanced and sophisticated, as she reflected her growing understanding of the power of narrative and the ability of storytelling to transcend cultural boundaries.

Anya's vibrant drawings, Mateo's detailed maps, and Sofia's handwritten folklore tales adorned the pages.

The project's influence extended beyond their immediate circle. Their success encouraged Jessica and her friends to share their stories with the broader community. They organized a storytelling event at the local library, inviting their neighbors and other children to take part.

The event was a resounding success. Jessica and her friends captivated children and adults alike with their stories, illustrations, and sheer enthusiasm. The event highlighted the transformative power of imagination and the importance of collaboration and cultural exchange. It served as a platform, fostering a sense of community and belonging.

As winter approached, painting the backyard in a blanket of white, Jessica knew the adventures would continue. The changing seasons would bring new possibilities, challenges, and opportunities to explore the limitless expanse of their imaginative world. Once a simple space, the backyard had become a stage for endless possibilities, a canvas for collaborative creativity, a testament to the power of imagination to transform the ordinary into the extraordinary. And Jessica, armed with her imagination and the support of her friends and community, was ready to embrace the new adventures that awaited. The enduring power of imagination had not transformed her world; it had connected her to a larger community, proving that creativity held the potential to bridge divides and enrich lives.

Chapter 49: Embracing the Future with Openness

A soft, white blanket of snow transformed the familiar backyard into a winter wonderland. The whispering willows, now draped in snow, seemed to hold their secrets even more closely. The oak tree, its branches heavy with the weight of the frozen world, looked like a majestic, snow-covered castle. However, Jessica pressed on. The change of season didn't diminish her imagination; it fueled it, igniting a fresh wave of creative energy. Instead of a haunted forest, she envisioned an ice kingdom, shimmering under the winter sun.

Her sketchbook, now filled with sketches of frost-covered flora and fauna, lay open on her bedroom windowsill. She'd drawn intricate ice sculptures, fantastical creatures with shimmering scales, icy breath, and winding pathways carved through the snowdrifts. She even sketched her hamster, Pip, bundled in a miniature snowsuit, acting as the brave guide through the icy wilderness. This wasn't a winter wonderland; it was a world of endless possibilities, each snowflake a unique story waiting to be told.

Mateo, Anya, and Sofia, excited by the transformation, joined her in creating this new realm of wonder. Ever the strategist, Mateo designed elaborate ice mazes, using snow blocks and frozen puddles as obstacles. Anya, her fingers nimble with frostbite-resistant gloves, painted vibrant murals onto the snow using natural pigments mixed with water, depicting winter sprites and magical snow creatures. Sofia's breath puffed out white clouds in the cold air, crafting enchanting tales of winter spirits and their icy adventures.

Inspired by a local winter festival, they extended their icy kingdom to the entire neighborhood. They carved ice sculptures in front of their houses, each telling a unique story — a playful penguin guarding a frozen treasure, a majestic snow leopard leaping through a crystalline arch, and a family of snow owls nestled in a frosty branch. They even created a miniature ice rink in the community park, transforming it into a magical skating rink where children could glide under the twinkling winter stars.

The local community welcomed their initiative. Mr. Kim, a skilled carpenter, built miniature ice houses for the neighborhood's children, each decorated with a unique winter-themed design.

Jessica's "Chronicles of the Backyard Kingdom" expanded to include the winter chapters, filled with detailed illustrations, maps, and stories. The journal wasn't a chronicle of their adventures; it became a collaborative artwork, a visual testament to the power of sharing warmly, weaving their stories into her world imagination. Anya's vibrant watercolor paintings depicted the magical creatures they created, while Mateo's detailed maps guided readers through their winter kingdom's icy pathways and hidden chambers. Sofia's handwritten tales of brave winter spirits and magical snowstorms filled the pages with enchantment.

Their collaborative storytelling extended beyond their immediate circle. They collaborated with the local school, transforming the schoolyard into a winter wonderland during the annual winter festival. Students contributed artwork inspired by their winter adventures, creating a kaleidoscope of snow-covered trees, icy castles, and glittering snowflakes. The culmination was a spectacular display of creativity, showcasing the power of sharing warmly, weaving their stories into her world's imagination to unite a community.

But the magic extended beyond visuals. Jessica's writing style strengthened, reflecting her growing maturity and understanding of the power of storytelling. Her narratives became richer and more sophisticated, incorporating various literary devices, like metaphors, similes, and personification, to create a more immersive and engaging reading experience. She blended fantasy with reality, using descriptive language to transport the reader into the world of icy adventures. She even started incorporating different narrative voices, giving each of her friends a chance to tell their own stories within the larger narrative.

Her writing style also became more diverse. To offer a broader view of their winter and the kingdom's unfolding events, she experimented with narrative styles, ranging from first-person to third-person omniscient. She incorporated elements of poetry and prose, using imagery and figurative language to create a more engaging and multi-sensory experience for the reader. Her weaving shifted from humor and lightheartedness to suspense and drama, depending on the situation being described. She developed a distinct authorial voice, characterized by her unique blend of imagination, empathy, and understanding of the human experience.

From a simple journal, "Chronicles of the Backyard Kingdom" blossomed into a collection of short stories, poems, and plays performed at the school's spring festival. The delightful blend of humor, drama, and fantasy in the play captivated the audience, transporting them into the whimsical world Jessica and her friends created. The play's success solidified Jessica's burgeoning talent as a storyteller, further empowering her to explore the boundless depths of her imagination.

As spring approached, melting the snow and ice, Jessica looked forward to new adventures, new possibilities. The changing seasons, once changes in weather, had become opportunities for creative exploration and community building. She realized that the true magic wasn't transforming her backyard, but transforming herself, as a writer, friend, and vibrant community member. She had learned that imagination was a tool not for individual joy but for fostering connections, building bridges between cultures, and celebrating the diverse tapestry of human experience.

This realization fueled her desire to continue her creative journey. She began working on a new project, a more extensive narrative that encompasses all the seasons and focuses on friendship, collaboration, and intercultural understanding. This latest project, she felt, would become an accurate reflection of her growth as a writer and her developing knowledge of the power of collaborative storytelling. She envisioned a book that would entertain its readers and inspire them to explore their boundless imaginations, connect with their communities, and celebrate the rich tapestry of human experience. Her experiences taught her that the most incredible adventures are not just about discovering new worlds, but also about finding oneself in the process of creating them.

Chapter 50: A Call to Adventure for Readers

Long shadows stretched across Jessica's backyard, cast by the sun, a warm golden orb in the spring sky. The snow had melted, leaving behind damp earth that smelled of fresh growth and the promise of new adventures. The whispering willows, no longer burdened by snow, swayed in the breeze, their leaves whispering secrets only they understood. Once a majestic snow-covered castle, the oak tree stood tall and proud, its leaves unfurling like emerald flags in the gentle wind. Perched on her now-dry swing set, Jessica smiled, the sensation of contentment washing over her. The winter kingdom, while magical, was now a cherished memory. A chapter closed in the ongoing saga of her backyard adventures.

However, feeling accomplishment wasn't about the winter adventures, but about the journey itself — the journey of transforming a mundane backyard into extraordinary worlds, discovering hidden talents, and forming meaningful connections within her community. The transformation in her backyard mirrored her transformation. She'd begun as a girl with a vibrant imagination and a love for adventure, and she'd ended up as a confident young writer and storyteller, capable of weaving fantastical tales that captivated not only herself but her friends and her entire neighborhood.

She remembered the initial hesitations, the moments of self-doubt. Sometimes the creative process felt overwhelming, when the blank page seemed to mock her ambition. But she'd persevered, driven by an unwavering belief in herself and the power of her imagination. The support of her friends, Mateo, Anya, and Sofia, had been invaluable, their collaborative spirit fueling her creative fire.

The process hadn't been without its challenges. There were disagreements about plotlines, creative differences, and the occasional artistic tantrum. However, these moments of friction strengthened their bond and honed their skills. They learned to compromise, appreciate diverse perspectives, and celebrate each other's successes. True collaboration, they understood, valued individual contributions, rather than enforcing uniformity.

The community's involvement added another layer of depth and meaning to their creative endeavors. Mr. Kim's carpentry skills, Mrs. Rodriguez's storytelling prowess, and Mrs. Chen's literary expertise played pivotal roles in shaping their winter wonderland. Their participation showed the importance of community engagement and the transformative power of sharing warmly, weaving their stories into her world creativity to turn ordinary spaces into extraordinary realms of wonder. It reinforced the idea that creativity wasn't a solitary pursuit, but a collective endeavor that brought people together and enriched their lives in countless ways.

The "Chronicles of the Backyard Kingdom" wasn't a chronicle of their adventures; it was a tapestry woven with threads of collaborative creativity and intercultural understanding. The journal served as a testament to their collective imagination, a physical manifestation of their creative journey. Each page held not only their stories but also their personalities, hopes, and dreams. It was a testament to the transformative power of sharing warmly, weaving their stories into her world experiences and the joy of collaborative storytelling.

As Jessica looked towards the future, she realized that the "Chronicles of the Backyard Kingdom" was not the end of her adventures, but a mere beginning. The skills she'd developed, the friendships she'd forged, and the lessons she'd learned would be a foundation for future creative endeavors. She envisioned creating stories to entertain and inspire young readers to explore their imaginations, discover the extraordinary adventures hidden in their everyday lives, and embrace the transformative power of collaborative storytelling.

And so, she turned the last page of her winter chronicles, sensing a sense of closure and an overwhelming excitement for what lay ahead. Spring had arrived, promising new beginnings, fresh perspectives, and endless possibilities. Once again, the backyard was ready for transformation, its canvas waiting to be painted with recent adventures, stories, and magical creations. This wasn't the end of a chapter; it was a call to adventure. A call not for Jessica, but for every young reader who held a spark of imagination within their hearts. The story of the Backyard Kingdom served as a blueprint, a guide for embarking on their journeys of creative exploration. The story revealed to readers that the most extraordinary adventures often live not in distant lands, but in familiar places, awaiting discovery through imaginative eyes.

Imagine your backyard, your room, your street. What secrets do they contain? Lurking, what fantastic creatures could there be? What thrilling journeys are yet to be uncovered? The answer, my young reader, lies within the realm of your imagination. Let your imagination run wild; you might be surprised at the wonders you discover.

You might discover a hidden world beneath your bed, a land populated by miniature creatures, engaging in their intricate lives. Perhaps your bookshelf transforms into a magical library, its shelves overflowing with enchanted books, each telling a unique tale of fantastical journeys and daring quests. Or your backyard becomes a sprawling jungle, teeming with exotic plants, singing birds, and mysterious creatures lurking in the shadows of the trees.

Jessica's journey is one to remember. Remember the winter kingdom, built not of snow and ice, but of shared stories and the unwavering belief in the power of imagination. Remember how she transformed her everyday life into an extraordinary adventure? You can do the same. The next time you stare out the window, wander through your neighborhood, or sit and dream, let your imagination take flight. Embrace your imagination; don't let fear stifle your creative spirit. Elevate the common to the exceptional; the everyday to the enchanting; the known for the fantastic.

This isn't about creating fantastical worlds; it's about discovering your unique voice and talent. It's about finding your inner spark, that unique creativity. Jessica's transformative power, yours too, elevates the mundane to the magical, crafting captivating and inspiring narratives. Share your experiences; there's no need to be afraid. Find your own Mateo, Anya, and Sofia—your friends, family, and community—to collaborate with, share your ideas, and celebrate your achievements.

Embrace the power of storytelling. It's a gift that connects us, transcends boundaries, and celebrates the diversity of human experience. Like Jessica, you can use your stories to build bridges between cultures.

Your journey of creative exploration might start in your backyard, like Jessica's, but where it will lead is up to you. Let your imagination be your guide, your compass, and your muse. Embrace the unexpected turns, celebrate the setbacks, and never underestimate the power of your boundless creativity. The world is waiting to hear your story. The adventures are waiting to unfold. So, my young reader, take a deep breath, unleash your imagination, and embark on your extraordinary adventure. You could be the one to write the most fantastic stories, yet unwritten. The world awaits your unique voice, creative spirit, and boundless imagination. Go forth and create your world, your kingdom, your magical masterpiece. The adventure begins now.

Acknowledgments

Thank you to my family and friends for their unwavering support and endless inspiration. Special thanks to my editor and Illustrator, Karen Shayler, for guiding and believing in this project. A huge thank you to all the young readers who inspire me daily to create worlds of wonder.

I would also like to thank all the members of The Explorers Club and The Royal Geographical Society. You have been a great inspiration and a driving force, and may this book inspire future explorations!

Author's Biography

Brett is a children's book author enthusiastic about creating playful and imaginative stories that spark a love for reading and adventure. With a background in fiction writing and a deep appreciation for the power of storytelling, Brett aims to create books that entertain and inspire young readers to explore their worlds and unleash their imaginations. When not crafting fantastical tales, Brett enjoys spending time outdoors, exploring the natural world, and discovering the magic hidden in everyday life. Brett is a member of the Explorers Club and the Royal Geographical Society.